Bicknell Family Association

The Bicknells and the Family Re-Union

At Weymouth, Massachusetts, September 22, 1880 - Addresses, poems

and speeches

Bicknell Family Association

The Bicknells and the Family Re-Union
At Weymouth, Massachusetts, September 22, 1880 - Addresses, poems and speeches

ISBN/EAN: 9783337158309

Printed in Europe, USA, Canada, Australia, Japan

Cover: Foto ©Andreas Hilbeck / pixelio.de

More available books at **www.hansebooks.com**

Bicknell

AND THE

FAMILY RE-UNION,

AT WEYMOUTH, MASSACHUSETTS,

SEPTEMBER 22, 1880.

ADDRESSES, POEMS AND SPEECHES.

BY THE PUBLICATION COMMITTEE,

FOR THE FAMILY.

BOSTON:
NEW ENGLAND PUBLISHING CO., PRINTERS.
1880.

PREFACE.

This little volume contains a brief statement of the formation and organization of the Bicknell Family Association, with an account of the family re-union at Weymouth, and the speeches, poem, and addresses of that occasion. We are indebted to Albion H. Bicknell, Esq., of Malden, Mass., for the beautiful family coat-of-arms, which faces the title page. This design belongs to the Bicknells of Spring Garden Terrace, London, and may properly be claimed as ours. The adoption of this particular crest and shield does not preclude the possible or the probable existence of other emblems in the possession of members of our own family, both in England and America. Its beauty and characteristics are worthy of special note. It is also proper to state that the poem is the joint product of Mrs. Ames and Alfred Bicknell, a proof that the poetical talent of the family is not confined by sex lines. Sharp critics may be able to discriminate between the products of the masculine and feminine mind.

It is earnestly desired that every person, who claims descent from Zachary Bicknell, or who has Bicknell blood of any kind in his veins, will join our Association. We also solicit names and facts, such as will help us in the future publication of a volume, which shall contain a complete and interesting history as well as genealogy of our whole family. To this end, every scrap of information, history, story and tradition should be written out at once, and sent to our family historian, Quincy Bicknell, Esq., Hingham, Mass. What is quickly done, is well done.

With fraternal greetings,

THOMAS W. BICKNELL,

Pres't B. F. A.

THE BICKNELLS.

HE Bicknell family is one of the oldest in America. So far as is now known, all of the name now living in this country, are traceable to Zachary and Agnes Bicknell, who, with their son John, and servant John Kitchin, sailed from England, in the spring of 1635, and landed at Wessagusets, now Weymouth, within the limits of Massachusetts Bay Colony, in the summer of that year, with the Rev. Joseph Hull and one hundred and one others, mostly from the counties of Somerset and Dorset in the southwest part of England.

The ship's record is as follows:

"ZACHARY BICKNELL aged 45 yeare.
AGNIS BICKNELL his wife aged 27 yeare.*
JNO. BICKNELL his sonne aged 11 yeare.
Jno. Kitchin his servaunt 23 yeare."

From this little family has sprung a numerous progeny, scattered over all parts of the country. In correspondence with a number of the family it was suggested that an Association be formed for social and genealogical purposes. The plan was promptly responded to by those of the family in and near the old home town, and as the result of the consultation, the following circular was prepared and sent to as many of the Bicknells and their descent as were then known to the subscribers.

---

* There is probably an error in the transcription of Agnes' age from the London records. The record of deaths in Braintree states that Agnes died in 1643, aged forty-eight years. If this be correct, she was thirty-seven years of age instead of twenty-seven in 1635, eight years prior to her death.

The Bicknells.

The BICKNELLS in the United States are all supposed to be descendants of

ZACHARY BICKNELL,

an English naval officer, who came to this country in 1635, and died in Weymouth in 1636, leaving a son JOHN, the ancestor of a large and very respectable posterity. As the BICKNELL name and family is a worthy and honored one, it seems very desirable that those who have a common ancestry should meet together for the purpose of comparing notes of the history of each branch of the family, and of forming an Association for personal acquaintance; and also to gather up such material, historical facts, and records as will be of general interest, hoping that they may then be put in permanent form for preservation. To this end a preliminary meeting is called to be held at the residence of WILLIAM E. BICKNELL, No. 43 Somerset Street, Boston, on Thursday Evening, December 11, 1879. You are cordially invited to be present, and are also requested to extend the invitation to all others of the BICKNELL name and descent who are interested in the objects herein stated. Please to signify to either of the undersigned, on the receipt of this circular, your willingness to co-operate in the movement and the probabilities as to your attendance. If you cannot be present, please communicate such facts concerning your own family history on the BICKNELL side as may be of interest and service in the proposed work. As soon as an organization is effected, a record of all the branches and members of the family, so far as may be received, will be made, and you will be advised from time to time touching the progress of the work, which we hope may result in a complete genealogy of our family in which so many are interested. Please address your reply to either of the undersigned as early as is practicable.

THOMAS W. BICKNELL,
16 Hawley Street.

WILLIAM E. BICKNELL,
43 Somerset Street.

ALFRED BICKNELL,
33 Milk Street.

BOSTON, Dec. 1, 1879.

In answer to the call for a meeting of the family to form an Association, the following persons assembled at the house of W. E. Bicknell, 43 Somerset street, Boston.

THOMAS W. BICKNELL,	Boston,	Massachusetts.
WILLIAM EMERY BICKNELL,	"	"
REBECCA J. BICKNELL,	"	"
GEORGE WATERS BICKNELL,	Lowell,	"
EDWIN A. WYMAN,	Leominster,	"
GEORGE F. BICKNELL,	Attleboro',	"
FRANCIS ADAMS BICKNELL,	North Weymouth,	"
AUGUSTUS M. BICKNELL,	" "	"
QUINCY BICKNELL,	Hingham,	"
CLARA BICKNELL WALKER,	Lynn,	"
ELLERY BICKNELL CRANE,	Worcester,	"
ALFRED BICKNELL,	Melrose,	"
SARAH J. BICKNELL,	"	"
MAUDE MARGARET BICKNELL,	"	"
EMILY RICHARDS BICKNELL,	Charlestown,	"
ROBERT T. BICKNELL,	East Weymouth,	"
ANNA M. BICKNELL HOLLAND,	Concord,	"

The meeting was called to order by Thomas W. Bicknell, who read letters received from the following persons (who were unable to be present), in answer to the call issued:

JAMES BICKNELL (age eighty-four), Stanwix, Oneida Co., New York.

WILLIAM BICKNELL (age seventy-six), Buckfield, Maine.

BROWNELL MANN BICKNELL, Sidney, Maine.

WILLIAM BICKNELL, No. 367 Dorchester street, South Boston, Mass.

HARRIET BICKNELL, Canton, Maine.

STEPHEN BICKNELL, North Weymouth, Mass.

WILLIAM S. BICKNELL, Bicknell, Indiana.

JAMES W. BICKNELL, Canton, Maine.

JOSEPH L. BICKNELL, 32 Green Street, Boston, Mass.

HOLLAND W. NOYES, Brockton, Mass.

WILLIAM H. BICKNELL, Providence, R. I.

GEORGE A. BICKNELL, Washington, D. C.

William E. Bicknell then offered the following plan of Association, which, after some discussion of the various articles, was adopted.

PLAN OF ASSOCIATION.

ARTICLE I. Our Society shall be known as "The Bicknell Family Association."

ARTICLE II. Its objects are, to promote social relations and larger acquaintanceship among the lineal descendants of Zachary Bicknell of Weymouth, Mass. (1635), and all other lines of the same name; to collect material for a complete genealogy and history of the Bicknell family; and to make such plans for family re-unions, publication of historic matter and other similar purposes as may be decided upon by the Association.

ARTICLE III. Any person of the Bicknell name or descent may become a member of the Association by signing the articles of Association.

ARTICLE IV. The officers shall be a President, a Vice-President from each State represented, a Recording Secretary, who shall also be Treasurer, a Corresponding Secretary, an Historian, and an Executive Committee which shall consist of five members in addition to the President and the two Secretaries, to be elected at the first meeting for organization and thereafter annually in the month of December of each year.

ARTICLE V. Meetings shall be held annually on the second Thursday in December and at other times at the call of the Executive Committee or on request of any three members presented in writing to the Secretary. Five persons shall constitute a quorum.

ARTICLE VI. Such By-Laws may be made and amended, as may be deemed necessary, at any regular meeting of the Association, and the Plan of Association may be changed at any regular meeting by a two-thirds vote of the members present, previous notice of the change to be made having been given to each member in writing.

After the adoption of the Articles of Association the following Officers were elected for the ensuing year:

PRESIDENT.

THOMAS W. BICKNELL, Boston.

VICE-PRESIDENTS.

WILLIAM BICKNELL,	Buckfield, Maine.
REV. D. H. BICKNELL,	Underhill, Vermont.
MRS. ANNA M. B. HOLLAND,	Concord, Mass.
EDWARD J. BICKNELL,	Providence, R. I.
JAMES BICKNELL,	Stanwix, N. Y.
CHARLES P. BICKNELL,	Philadelphia, Penn.

Hon. George A. Bicknell,	New Albany, Ind.
Henry G. Bicknell,	Chicago, Ill.
Dr. Charles H. Bicknell,	Beloit, Wis.
Anson D. Bicknell,	Humboldt, Iowa.
Charles F. Bicknell,	Carson City, Nevada.
David Bicknell,	East Orange, N. J.
A. J. Bicknell,	New York, N. Y.
Charles T. Bicknell,	Massillon, O.
Mrs. Emma Bicknell Love,	Hopewell, N. B., Can.
George R. Bicknell,	St. Louis, Mo.
Mrs. Olive B. Hayford,	Austin, Texas.
Henry A. Bicknell,	Big Oak Flat, Cal.
Luke H. Bicknell,	Gallatin, Tenn.
Mrs. Ella C. Morrison,	Minneapolis, Minn.
Zeb. Mead,	Parkersburg, W. Va.
Otis P. Bicknell,	Brookville, Kansas.
Peter Bicknell,	New Orleans, La.
C. C. Bicknell,	Cedar Springs, Mich.

RECORDING SECRETARY AND TREASURER.

Robert T. Bicknell, East Weymouth.

CORRESPONDING SECRETARY.

Alfred Bicknell, Boston.

HISTORIAN.

Quincy Bicknell, Hingham.

EXECUTIVE COMMITTEE.

THE PRESIDENT.

THE SECRETARIES.

William E. Bicknell,	Boston.
George F. Bicknell,	Attleboro'.
Ellery Bicknell Crane,	Worcester.
George W. Bicknell,	Lowell.
Clara B. Walker,	Lynn.

At this meeting, the subject of a family re-union at Weymouth, was discussed, in a social way, and it was unanimously agreed that such a meeting was most desirable. Later the following circular was mailed to a large number of our family, in various parts of the country, to which responses were received, favoring the purposes of the Association, and a meeting of the different branches of the family at Weymouth.

The Bicknell Family Association

Was formed at Boston, Mass., in December, 1879. Its object is to promote acquaintanceship and social relations among the different members of the family; also to collect material, with the endeavor to complete the genealogy of the family from the first ancestor, ZACHARY BICKNELL, who came from England, in 1635, and settled at Weymouth, Mass.

By the articles of Association, any of the Bicknell name or descent may become members by signing the articles or by requesting the Secretary to do so for them. The Annual Meeting for choice of officers is to be held at Boston, each year, in December.

It is proposed to hold a re-union of the family at Weymouth during the coming summer.

At present there are no membership fees; but to meet the expenses of Stationery, Printing and Postage, any sums the members may see fit to send the Treasurer will be thankfully received and judiciously expended.

We should be pleased to receive your name for membership; and also to have you send as the names of others of the family.

For the Executive Committee,

ALFRED BICKNELL, *Corresponding Sec'y.*

ROBERT T. BICKNELL, *Treasurer.*

BOSTON, Feb. 2, 1880.

At a later meeting, held at Mr. Bicknell's, 43 Somerset street, Boston, Jan. 26, at which fourteen of the family were present, it was proposed that the meeting of the family be held at Weymouth, in June, 1880, and the whole matter was referred to the Executive Committee for their decision. At that meeting, Mr. E. B. Crane, of Worcester, read a paper on " The Coat-of-Arms " of the Bicknell Family, and presented a colored drawing of the emblems of the Bicknells of Spring Garden Terrace, London, as those to be recommended for adoption. Mr. T. W. Bicknell gave an account of "The Bicknell Name and its Corruptions." At a meeting of the Association May 27, the Executive Committee proposed that the family gathering be held at Weymouth, on Wednesday, September 22, 1880, and the following committees were chosen :

On ENTERTAINMENT — The Executive Committee.

On FINANCE — Alfred Bicknell, Ellery B. Crane and R. T. Bicknell.

The following persons were named to perform parts at the re-union :

The Address of Welcome — The President, Boston.
A Brief Family Story — Quincy Bicknell, Hingham.
The Historical Address — George A. Bicknell, M. C., Indiana.
The Poem — Mrs. A. H. Ames, Columbia, Penn.
Toast-Master — Zachariah L. Bicknell, Weymouth.

The following circular, setting forth the main features of the proposed re-union, was afterwards widely circulated.

Bicknell Family Association.

(Organized December, 1879.)

Thos. W. Bicknell, President,   R. T. Bicknell, Sec'y and Treas.
16 Hawley Street.   200 Devonshire Street.
Alfred Bicknell, Corresponding Sec'y.

33 Milk St., Boston, July 1, 1880.

To all persons of the "Bicknell" name or descent, Greeting:

A Re-union of the members of our family will be held under the auspices of this Association, at

Weymouth, Mass., Wednesday, September 22, 1880.

It has been thought by the members of our Association that it would be eminently pleasant and profitable to hold a general meeting of our Family,— one of the oldest and most respectable in our country,— in this town, where nearly two hundred and fifty years ago our common ancestor,

ZACHARY BICKNELL,

(the first settler of our name in America) planted the family from which has sprung the numerous progeny now scattered from Ocean to Ocean, and from the Lakes to the Gulf.

Suitable arrangements are being made to interest and entertain our friends and we hope and expect that representatives will be present from many States. It is proposed to spend the day on this historic ground, visiting the several points of particular interest, and making and renewing acquaintanceship with each other. The meeting of welcome will take place at the Church, at which, the President of our Association (now in Europe) will be present and give us an historical address, including such information as he is able to gather while abroad touching our English Ancestry. The Hon. George A. Bicknell, M. C., from Indiana, is expected to be present, and will address the meeting, and there will be other exercises, including music, toasts, addresses and a poem, by members of our family. A dinner will be served, which we intend to make a very enjoyable feature of the occasion.

The expenses of the day will be very moderate, being simply for carfare from Boston and return, and dinner. In order to know how many to provide for, it is very desirable to know, approximately, how many will attend, and you are therefore requested to advise either of the undersigned of your intentions. The place of meeting is on the South Shore Branch of the Old Colony Railroad, about twelve miles from Boston, and a part of the day will be spent on an eminence commanding an extensive view of Massachusetts Bay and surroundings. As there are no hotels near the place of meeting, it will be necessary to return to Boston at night. In case you cannot attend we shall be pleased to receive any communication you may choose to make, to be read if time permits.

As we have the addresses of only a small portion of the members of our family, we hope each one receiving this notice will circulate the same as fully as possible. Any inquiries or suggestions may be addressed to either of the undersigned.

Thos. W. Bicknell, 16 Hawley Street, Boston.	
Wm. E. Bicknell, 43 Somerset Street, "	*Committee*
Robt. T. Bicknell, 200 Devonshire St., "	*of*
Z. L. Bicknell, East Weymouth, or	*Arrangements.*
Alfred Bicknell, 33 Milk Street, "	

As the time of the meeting drew near, the Committee of Arrangements prepared the following programme of the proceedings at Weymouth.

BICKNELL FAMILY ASSOCIATION.

ORGANIZED, DECEMBER, 1879.

Thos. W. Bicknell, Pres't,   Robt. T. Bicknell, Sec'y and Treas.,
16 Hawley Street.   200 Devonshire Street.

Alfred Bicknell, Corresponding Secretary,

33 Milk Street, Boston, Mass

1635.  1880.

To all persons of the "Bicknell" name or descent, Greeting:

OF THE MEMBERS OF OUR FAMILY

Will be held, under the auspices of our Association,

—AT—

Weymouth, Mass., Wednesday, Sept. 22, 1880.

It has been thought that it would be both pleasant and profitable to hold a general meeting of our family — one of the oldest and most respectable in the country — in the old town, where nearly two hundred and fifty years ago, our common ancestor,

ZACHARY BICKNELL,

(the first settler of our name in America) planted the family from which has sprung the numerous progeny now scattered from Ocean to Ocean, and from the Lakes to the Gulf.

That the day may be made most valuable, in its social and historical aspects, to all who shall assemble, the Committee have adopted the following as the general Programme.

Programme.

MEETING OF WELCOME.

The Members of the Family and Invited Guests will meet at the Methodist Episcopal Church, East Weymouth, at 11 o'clock, A. M.

Order of Exercises.

VOLUNTARY ON THE ORGAN.

MUSIC.

(Kindly furnished by a Volunteer Choir.)

READING OF THE SCRIPTURES AND PRAYER,

By REV. GEO. W. BICKNELL, of Lowell, Mass.,

Chaplain of the day.

ADDRESS OF WELCOME,

By THOMAS W. BICKNELL, of Boston, President of the Family Association.

BRIEF HISTORY OF OUR FAMILY,

By QUINCY BICKNELL, of Hingham, Historian of the Association.

MUSIC.

ADDRESS,

By Hon. GEO. A. BICKNELL, M. C., of Indiana.

POEM,

By Mrs. A. H. (BICKNELL) AMES, of Columbia, Penn.

ORIGINAL HYMN.

(Written expressly for the occasion.)

BENEDICTION.

Dinner, Toasts, and Speeches.

At the conclusion of the preceding exercises, there will be an opportunity for personal introductions and social intercourse. At One o'clock *precisely*, DINNER will be served in the Vestry (the use of which for this purpose has been most kindly granted by the Trustees of the Church), by a well-known Boston Caterer. Toasts and after-dinner Speeches will follow this entertainment, in which it is expected that a large number of the FAMILY will take part,— Z. L. BICKNELL, Esq., of East Weymouth, acting as TOAST MASTER for the occasion.

Visits.

At three o'clock, visits will be made to the site of ZACHARY BICKNELL'S House in 1636; to "KING OAK HILL," where a fine land and sea view can be obtained; and to the ANCIENT CHURCH and CEMETERY, where the first BICKNELLS worshipped and were buried; and to other points of interest made DEAR to the HEARTS of RIGHT LOYAL DESCENDANTS.

To this social family gathering are invited all of the BICKNELL name and descent, and those connected by marriage, or otherwise, who desire to participate in these festivities. All members of the family receiving this notice are requested to act on the Committee of Invitation, and to extend this notice to all interested within their circles of acquaintance. We hope to enjoy a large gathering of our name and kin, and letters already received point to new and extended social relations of which all may be proud.

IMPORTANT ITEMS.

In order to meet the expenses of the occasion, including Dinner, Printing, etc., the price of Tickets for the Dinner is fixed at $1.00 each; and, that proper provision may be made to meet the wants of all in attendance, the Committee must know as early as Sept. 15 how many expect to attend. We therefore enclose a card, on which you will please write the names of those expecting to be present from your family and neighborhood, and also for how many dinner-tickets you and they will be responsible.

TRAINS TO AND FROM BOSTON.

Trains leave the Old Colony Depot, on Kneeland Street, at 7.35 and 11 A.M., stopping at both the North and East Weymouth Stations; and at 9.35, stopping at Braintree only, where carriages will connect for East Weymouth in time for the exercises at the Church.

Return trains leave North and East Weymouth at 4.25 and 6.15 P.M.

Free Return Tickets will be given by the Railroad Company, from Weymouth to Boston, to all paying the regular fare from Boston.

Friends who may be unable to attend, but who desire to contribute towards the expenses of the gathering, may send funds to Robt. T. Bicknell, *Treas.*, No. 200 Devonshire St., Boston. All are invited to send autograph letters and photographs, to be preserved as a memorial of this first meeting.

It is hoped that a complete genealogy of the family will be eventually prepared, and an expression of your interest in this matter is solicited.

In case you cannot attend, we shall be pleased to receive any communication you may choose to make, to be read if time permits.

As we have the addresses of only a small portion of the members of our family, we hope each one receiving this notice will gather the names and post-office addresses of those known to him, and mail the same to our *Historian* or *Corresponding Secretary.*

Any inquiries or suggestions may be addressed to either of the undersigned.

Thos. W. Bicknell, 16 Hawley Street, Boston.
Wm. E. Bicknell, 43 Somerset Street, "
Robt. T. Bicknell, 200 Devonshire St., "
Z. L. Bicknell, East Weymouth, or
Alfred Bicknell, 33 Milk Street, "

} *Committee of Arrangements.*

ADDRESS OF WELCOME.

BY THOMAS W. BICKNELL, PRESIDENT OF THE BICKNELL FAMILY
ASSOCIATION.

LADIES AND GENTLEMEN, BRETHREN OF THE BICKNELL
NAME AND DESCENT:

It is my happy duty and privilege to welcome you all
home to this glad family re-union. Two hundred and
forty-five years have passed since Zachary Bicknell,
his wife Agnes, their son John, and servant John
Kitchin landed on the soil of Weymouth, then called
by the name of Wessaguseus. Not far from the spot
where we now are, they planted their home and set up
their household gods, fifteen years after the settlement of the Pilgrims at Plymouth, and five after the founding of Boston by the
Puritans. The sifted seed wheat of Old England found congenial
soil on these Eastern shores of Massachusetts Bay, and from that
first planting in 1635 a single seed corn has multiplied till it fills
the whole earth.

That Zachary and Agnes were a devoted pair, is seen in the fact
that they came together, with their all, to share the joys and trials
of pioneer life, two and a half centuries ago. That they were
courageous souls, is shown by their readiness to face the perils of
a rough sea voyage, and the rougher hardships of a life in the

wilderness. not yet redeemed from the savages. That they came to stay. is manifest from the fact that they brought their only son and servant. and built their house on their arrival. That they were of religious stuff. is evidenced by the fact that with their pastor. Joseph Hull. they helped to form the Old North Church of Weymouth. That our ancestors labored and suffered to build this ancient heritage, is certain when we remember that toil and sickness brought our grandfather Zachary to his dying bed within a year after his arrival ; and that our grandmother. Agnes. was a woman of strong character and personal attractions is manifest. since she became the wife of Richard Rocket. within a twelvemonth after her husband's death.

Now it is a matter of some pride to *belong* to the *human family*, but far greater to be a member of *the Bicknell family*. and as this is BICKNELL DAY. the *red letter day* of our calendar. we propose to do a little family boasting among ourselves. and let the outside world wag along one day without our special help. Of one thing we are sure. it will see and appreciate our value by to-morrow.

Eight cities vied with each other in claiming Homer as theirs. More than eight cities have sought and claimed the Bicknell name, and to-day, we have come hither from Maine, whither our NOAH with his ark of souls floated on the tide of Northern Emigration, till his feet found dry land among the hills of the Pine Tree State ; from Rhode Island. whither ZACHARY the second. his wife Hannah, their six sons and daughters pitched their tents on "The westward end of Swansea" in the first emigration toward the great West ; from Connecticut. whither ZACHARY the *third* and JAMES found their home and made their graves ; from Central Massachusetts whither JAPHET and his godly company sought the Golden Fleece in well tilled farms and growing herds ; from Vermont and New Hampshire, where PETER and his descendants sought Fortune's service in his removal from Barrington to the fertile valleys of the Green Mountain State ; from New York. whither a branch of our Connecticut Yankees immigrated more than a century ago. with their goods packed on a single wagon. and the whole company and load drawn by oxen : from Pennsylvania. where Maine sent her sons to make their fortune of coal and iron ; from Ohio and Indiana. where great men grow and where politicians have a lively occupation ; from Illinois and Wisconsin. from Iowa and Utah and California and from — everywhere — we have come home to see the old homestead, to shake the warm hands of each other. and of the girls and boys, who have with loving hearts and faithful service kept the household goods unharmed, the household name untarnished, and the ancestral graves crowned with honors.

OLD WEYMOUTH, clad in her beautiful autumn array, greets us. Her three hundred and fifty Bicknells and their children, in whose veins flows good Bicknell blood, interlaced with that of the Dyers, Richards, Turners, Truphants, Bates', Merchants, Tirrells, Salisburys, Goodspeeds, Frenchs, Mardens, Pratts, Reeds, Torreys, Newtons, Rices, Raymonds, Spilsteds, Orcutts and others, greet us to-day, and as face answers to face in water, so the Bicknell recognition is manifest, even though the visage bears not the well recognized Roman beak, the eye has not the touch of the pencilled blue, and the frame has not reached the regulation height of six feet.

Brothers and sisters from far and near, do you realize the fact that you are at home to-day? You have long desired to see the sites which this day greet you, to see the men and women of our blood who have joined in this joyful assemblage. Imagination has often travelled the spaces which separate us from these sacred family scenes and has pictured the homestead of old Zachary and Agnes, the house they built, the land they cultivated, the church in which they worshipped and the graves where they sleep. It is a precious privilege that as pilgrims we may now gather at the shrine of our fathers, and in the spirit of devout worshippers gather something of the inspiration which led them to build here an edifice, better than their fancies dreamed. For look where you will, the Bicknell blood has nowhere done dishonor to the Bicknell ancestry, and bating the common frailties, which prove us genuine descendants of an earlier common stock, we have whereof to boast.

Of Goodman Zachary and Goodwife Agnes, we must read their history between the lines of the few historic facts which have come to us. Of good English, and if we may credit the tradition, of Scandinavian blood, we find the Bicknells in 1635 as to-day, dwellers in the County of Somerset in the southwest of England. Most probably from the old town of Taunton came our ancestors to join the Weymouth Company, under the pastoral care of Rev. Joseph Hull. Dissenters by faith, feeling at home the heavy hand of social and political persecution, they looked to the new world as a quiet resting place for faith, if not for fortune. Troublous times were behind them, but do you not count them brave to face

the hardships which beset their onward way? To-day it is a
march from want to luxury, from political inequality to equal
rights, to emigrate from European to American shores, but we
should never forget to admire the real heroism which brought the
early families of New England from circumstances of comparative
comfort at home, to endure the sad and trying experiences of a
new civilization. Nought but good blood and good names came out
into this pioneer life on the eastern shores of our rugged New
England, and so when an ancestry dates back as does ours, nearly
two and one-half centuries, we have occasion for just pride in that
sublime purpose which inspired to a better future, an unbending
will which yielded to no obstacles, a love stronger than adamant,
which bound husband to wife, parent to child, friend to friend.

Mrs. Hemans may have had our own ancestry in mind, when she
wrote these imperishable lines :—

> "There was woman's fearless eye,
>   Lit by her deep love's truth ;
> There was manhood's brow serenely high,
>   And the fiery heart of youth.
>
> " What sought they thus afar,
>   Bright jewels of the mine?
> The wealth of seas, the spoils of war?
>   They sought a Faith's pure shrine !
>
> " Aye, call it holy ground,
>   The soil where first they trod !
> They have left unstained what there they found
>   Freedom to worship God."

We often speak of a child as a chip of the old block. As we
have not the ancestral block at hand, we must look at the family
chips to get a fair likeness, and of some of these specimens, and their
characteristics I may speak to-day. In general, however, I may say
that the American Bicknells have been a busy set of fellows. "No
drones in our hive !" says one of our name in the West, and so
say we all of us. I don't believe that Zachary or Agnes had a lazy
bone in their bodies ; if so, that blood ceased to perpetuate itself.
We have been a hard working people. Toilers in agricultural and
mechanical life in the main, we have earned our bread by the warm
sweat of sunburned faces and hard-handed toil ; and there the
honor lies. Look up and down the land and find me if you can a

Bicknell name, dependent save through personal infirmities or sad misfortune. David said, "Once I was young, now I am old, yet I have never seen the righteous forsaken or his seed begging bread." Substitute *Bicknell* for *righteous* and the quotation is apt for our family. Agur's golden mean of neither poverty nor riches seems to have been the ambition of most of our name, probably remembering the proverb that a *good name* is better than great riches. With honest industry has been coupled temperance and virtue. Look through our annals and see how few, if any, have yielded to the seductions of vice and intemperance. In my own inquiries, I have never found a name dishonored by habitual drunkenness or by criminal intent. This is our proudest boast to-day, that for two hundred and forty-five years we have no family name, whose record we could not willingly hear without a blush, at this our glad anniversary. Great names, as the world counts greatness, have often descended through base deeds, but the highest honor of our title is that its fine gold has not become tarnished by low characters and dishonorable lives. A characteristic letter from an Indiana Bicknell, one of the lost tribe through North Carolina, says, "I never heard of a Bicknell being arrested, put in jail or in prison in my life. I never knew a Bicknell that was an infidel and I hope I never may." And adds still further, "they all vote the Republican ticket." We fear the returns were not all in at that writing. And this suggests the characteristic of high moral and religious sentiments as a golden thread running through our whole family history. Zachary and Agnes were religious people, Puritans, if you please.—God bless the name. John was a brother in the Old North Church, and looked after its outward as well as spiritual welfare. In 1661, so say the town records, "Brother Bicknell was allowed three pounds for making the Meeting House t-i-t-e." If Bro. Bicknell was as faithful in his spiritual services in keeping the Meeting House *tight*, he certainly was worthy of a royal reward. So far as I know, a practical Christian life has characterized the family from John through all his descendants till this very hour, and wherever the name exists, it stands as the synonym of godly living and doing. Of one town settled by Bicknells of the third generation, namely, Barrington, R. I., it was set off from Old Swansea to enable the people "to settle and maintain a pious, learned and orthodox ministry, for the good of us and our posterity," and Zachariah the 2nd. not only signed but probably wrote the petition to the General Court for the separation.

Of the church membership of our family I have now no means of knowing. nor do I know how large a number have held the honorable offices of deacon, Sabbath-school superintendent, etc. That we have. and have had a pious and learned ministry is evidenced in this as well as in past generations. The oldest now living is Rev. James Bicknell, of Oneida county, N. Y., a Baptist clergyman, eighty-five years of age. He is a man of remarkable talents, and it is said that his influence in his denomination in New York is still powerful. Rev. L. W. Bicknell, of Indiana, is also a Baptist preacher. Rev. Dennis H. Bicknell, of Vermont, and Rev. I. J. Bicknell, of Indiana. represent us among Methodists. Rev. Wm. M. Bicknell, of Rowe, Mass., is a talented Unitarian clergyman. Rev. E. A. Wyman, Ph. D., is a preacher and author. Rev. Geo. W. Bicknell, of Lowell, our chaplain, is a prominent and esteemed Universalist pastor and teacher. Rev. J. R. Bicknell, son of our distinguished guest and statesman, Hon. Geo. A. Bicknell. is an Episcopal rector in Indiana. There are several others. clergymen in the Congregational, Presbyterian and other denominations. More might be said of those who are doing *good preaching*, but what shall we say of the legion who are doing *good practising?*

It is quite a remarkable fact. that. while some of our New England Bicknells held slaves. they were at a very early date given their freedom. and some of the family name have been noted abolitionists. when it cost something to stand on that side of the question of human rights.

My own great-grandfather, dying in 1750, gave to his wife, his negro man Dick. and female negro child Rose, to serve her during her natural life. and at her death to receive, each one hundred pounds and their freedom papers. If you find anywhere the Bicknell name under a black skin. do not refer it to a remote pre-adamic ancestry. or to a change of skin under climatic influence, but to the choice of the Bicknell name as its patronymic when liberated from slavery. Of the North Carolina Bicknells, Samuel was a large slave-owner.

Though the Bicknells have been unambitious in the line of public life and honors. the family has had its full share in the important trusts of civil society. They have not rudely sought, nor lightly

declined their share of duty and responsibility. The records of
every town where our name has existed, show the various positions of official service filled by members of our family. Our
ancestor John was a deputy from Weymouth in the General Court
of Massachusetts Bay in 1677-8 and his descendants, among
whom is our honored toast-master, have often represented this
town in the State legislature. The same honors have been borne
by our name in other States. Joshua Bicknell, my grandfather,
was a member of the Rhode Island Legislature in both branches for
several years, and won the sobriquet, "Old Aristides." He was
also a judge of the Supreme Court of Rhode Island for many years
before and until his death. One son was Senator and Representative for several years, and two of his grandsons have held the
office of Commissioner of Public Schools of Rhode Island. I hold
in my hand the fine face of a Bicknell who represents us and his
constituency in the Iowa Legislature.

The Bicknell name has been enrolled twice on the Congressional
Records. Bennet Bicknell, of New York, represented his district
in an early Congress, and we have the honor of having present with
us, as orator of the day, one of the leaders of the present House of
Representatives at Washington, in the person of Judge and Hon.
George Augustus Bicknell, of New Albany, Ind., who represented
his district in the last and present Congresses, and we trust will
continue to hold the place so honorably filled, for years to come.
We will promise him a large Bicknell vote, though holding different
politic creeds.

Of lawyers we have had several honest names: Hon. Geo. A.,
of Indiana, Emory O. and Edward E., of Boston, Anson D., of
Iowa, John, of California, Leonard, of Vermont, and several
others, not of the Bicknell name, are fair specimens of the legal
limb of the family. Of medicine we have had little need; a
healthy stock, we have "thrown physic to the dogs and after it
the doctor." We have raised a few medicine men to look out for
other poor sick sinners, among whom we will name Dr. George
Bicknell, of Wisconsin, Dr. Joshua Bicknell Chapin, of Rhode
Island, and a few others. So you see we are little given to
quackery.

In art we have a distinguished name whose health detains from
this joyful union. I refer to Albion H. Bicknell, of Malden, Mass.
His historic painting of Lincoln at Gettysburg has made for him a

fame more than national. and he has on his canvas a painting of
rare merit, which when finished. will be classed among the gems of
American art.   Of the great English art patron, Elhanan Bicknell,
of London, I would speak, were we not favored by the presence
of one of our English cousins of the Bicknell name to speak of
him.

In microscopy, Science has just lost a bright name in the death
of Edwin Bicknell, of Lowell.

But in business life and in the pursuits which add to the sum of
human happiness our names are found in distinguished retirement
and comfortable independence. Z. L. Bicknell is the man of all
work in Weymouth; Alfred and William and Joseph represent
our Boston men of affairs; A. J., Joseph George and David are
our representatives in New York; Edward and Joshua in Providence; E. B. Crane and others in Worcester; Joseph Y., in Buffalo as Superintendent of the Buffalo General Hospital; Henry E.
and others in Chicago, and here and there, up and down the country are men and women of our name and descent. industrious,
prudent, good natured, hospitable, temperate, truthful. independent, morally courageous, generous, man-loving, God-fearing people.

In the teaching profession. we have had a host of names both of
men and women. One of our Vermont families alone has had nine-
teen teachers, among whom was Simeon, a noted man in his day,
and that recent. Two of our family have filled the office of State
Commissioners of public schools in Rhode Island, with some degree
of credit to the name. In literary life, we have in England and
America, a few names as authors and poets.   In fact, the poetic
vein is a strong Bicknell trait. The poems and poets of the day
will attest my assertion.

But who is equal to the task of speaking of those of us not
bearing the Bicknell name? I fear the world itself would not contain the books that might be written. Their name is legion, for
they are many. The roll call would waste the swift hours of this
grand day. We'll talk of these to each other, and be proud that
such a progeny has sprung from so pure and noble a stock. We
come from many homes where peace, comfort and sweet hospitality
abound. to behold how good and how pleasant it is for brethren to
dwell together in unity. Would that we could, by some magic
voice, summon Zachary and Agnes and John, that first little

family of Weymouth in 1635, to our social re-union. Not in form, but in fact, they still live in you and in me. Their dust is on yonder hillside, but their lives projected into the centuries, reappear in an intelligent, an industrious, and a happy offspring. Like the grave of Moses on Nebo, no stone marks their sepulchre, but a living monument rises day after day, without the sound of hammer or chisel, wrought by noble resolve, by steadfast purpose or heroic will. It is fashioned by many artists and artisans here and there under "The Great Taskmaster's eye," and will appear when he who sees the perfect pattern, shall declare the work finished and complete, fit for the Master's eye. Brothers and sisters of all names, one to-day by a common family bond, we greet you in the name of our Association; we welcome you to the festivities of the hour, to the large family outlook you will take to-day, and to the events which will soon pass into pleasant memories. Draw faith, courage and inspiration from our re-union, and return refreshed and blessed. Bicknells by name and blood, proud in your origin and in your family history, welcome, thrice welcome to the feast! May the day be one of happy experiences and of blessed memories to you all.

A BRIEF FAMILY STORY.

BY QUINCY BICKNELL, FAMILY HISTORIAN.

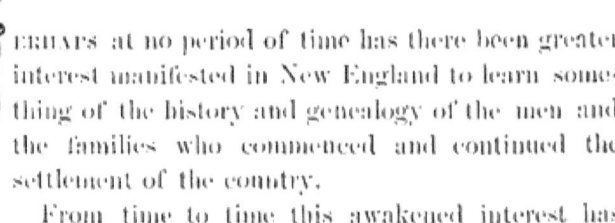 ERHAPS at no period of time has there been greater interest manifested in New England to learn something of the history and genealogy of the men and the families who commenced and continued the settlement of the country.

From time to time this awakened interest has found expression in gathering together the widely scattered descendants, upon or near the ancestral homes and in published genealogies of many of these families. These gatherings are valuable in their social aspects, and the publications important as they become a part of our history.

Whether we look at the results which have attended the settlement of New England or to the causes which impelled the men and women who made the settlement to leave their homes of comfort and civilization to encounter the perils of the ocean passage and the wilderness, and to endure all the privations attendant upon the work of subduing it, we have ample reason to warrant the interest we feel in the retrospection.

The immediate cause of this settlement was the development upon English soil of the man and the character we call Puritan, who though subjected to harsh criticism and much censure, for imperfections, belonging to humanity in its best estate, yet when we contemplate the fulness of the character, stands out like the pyramids among the sands of the desert, dwarfing every surrounding object.

The commercial interests of England had been stirred into an unwonted degree of activity and enterprise by the discovery of America, and the maritime enterprise engendered thereby,—wealth from this source had given learning and culture to a class of people, who for years had been immersed in ignorance, and had caused a general spread of knowledge among the common people.

For a generation previous to the settlement of New England, this increase of knowledge among the people had taken the direction of inquiry and agitation, into the relation of the individual to the higher concerns affecting his relation to his Maker and the more subordinate but still highly important one to the State.

He lived among the observances of a religious ritual, guarded by the flaming sword of the law, and so encumbered with material observances as to hinder rather than to help the soul to find its approach to the throne of divine mercy.

He essayed to strip from the temples of worship all these gorgeous emblems and dared to come into the immediate presence of his Maker, humbled in dust in view of his own unworthiness, but strong in his appreciation of the worth of the individual soul, in view of the sacrifice made for its atonement and redemption.

In the severity of his logic he carried his ideas of the worth of the human soul to matters of State and claimed that human institutions of government had the sanction of divine authority only as they were made to subserve the best and highest interest of man, and from this thought he developed the idea of a Commonwealth.

The attempt to make practical the Puritan idea of church and state in England, raised an issue that culminated in the civil war, led to the beheading of Charles the First, the destruction of the attempted Commonwealth, the imperialism of Cromwell and the restoration of the monarchy.

Before these issues were brought to the stern arbitrament of war, some of the more intelligent and adventuresome of these men sought another means for the solution of the problem, and that was by emigration, and establishing elsewhere a Commonwealth.

To obtain chartered privileges for this especial purpose was impossible, and the ingenuity and daring by which the purpose was accomplished stand among the highest acts of moral heroism the world has witnessed.

A company chartered for the purpose of forming plantations in New England, was the instrument by which they proposed and through which they did enter upon their great work. The plantations which these companies were supposed to establish were the usual ones attendant upon commercial and fishing pursuits, and made for purposes of commercial gain. They were authorized to choose their officers for the proper management of their affairs and to make suitable laws for their government not repugnant to the laws of England.

The act of daring was the transfer of the whole government of this company and its charter to New England, and out of this small beginning has grown up the Commonwealth, under whose broad shield of government we now assemble and to the very name of which we cling with venerated affection, leaving to our sister communities the appellation of States.

The character of this emigration induced others holding similar sentiments in England to join them, especially as the power of the mother country was directed with increased severity and vigilance to suppress them. This vigilance was directed to the enrolment of all those proposing to leave England, and to requiring the oath of supremacy.

To this act of enrolment we are indebted for the record which gives the time and place of departure of Zachary Bicknell, from England, with the members of his family and their respective ages, Weymouth being the point of embarkation, with wife Agnes twenty-seven years old, he being forty-five, son John eleven, and servant John Kitchin, twenty-three. They came in 1635.

He came with the Rev. Mr. Hull and his company, and here they made their home. Others had been here before them, and soon after a considerable number left, among them the Rev. Mr. Newman and many with him, and went to Rehoboth. Some remained and, with those who joined them, commenced the settlement of this town of Weymouth. Soon after the church was formed and then with the organization of church and town, the people entered upon the work they had before them.

They built themselves houses of rude construction, barely sheltering them from the inclemencies of the seasons, felled the forests that they might have food and raiment, built their meeting-house, and by its side the humbler school-house, that knowledge might not die out among them, and freed from the impediments to their spiritual comforts, they entered upon a career of progress, with such success that to-day if we are asked for the results, we answer in the language of Sir Christopher Wren, "Look around."

Among these early immigrants, was Zachary Bicknell, but who and what he was we have at present limited means of determining, but it is fair to infer that he was in sympathy with the spirit that led the emigration, and that he was a man of substance as were many of his associates ; and more particularly so as he was accompanied by a young man as a servant.

Many of the young men bound themselves to a period of service to defray the expenses of their emigration, and from this class have sprung some of the best families of New England, and of this class this young man was not an exception ; for we find that John Kitchin was in Salem in 1610, freeman, 1613. He was a shoemaker and had a family of seven children of whom Robert, the youngest, was a merchant and ship-owner in Salem, and his son Robert[3], a student at Harvard College, died the twentieth of September, 1716, more than a century before any of the descendants of his master enjoyed the advantages of college instruction.

Zachary Bicknell died the year following his arrival, having built a house upon land granted by the town. This house and land was sold the next year to Wm. Reed,—as appears by an order of court affirming the sale,—for the General Court under date of March, 1636, ordered, "That William Reade, having bought the house and twenty acres of land at Weymouth, unfenced, which was Zachary Bicknell's, for seven pounds, thirteen shillings and four pence, of Richard Rocket and wife, is to have the sale confirmed by the child when he cometh of age, or else the child to allow such costs as the court shall think meet." It seems that Agnes or Annie, as the name differently appears, married again soon after the death of her husband, Zachary Bicknell. She was probably his second wife and not the mother of his son John, as an inspection of the ages of these several persons would seem to show. (See page 5, Note.)

The land which Wm. Reed bought of Zachary Bicknell's estate, remained in the Reed family for many years, and we have one among us to-day who remembers the last of that name who owned and occupied the land, so that we are able to identify the exact

spot where Zachary Bicknell rested and established his home, so
soon to be determined and ended by his death. It is on Middle
street, and is the estate of the late Sylvanus Bates, deceased.
A flag marks the spot to-day, and it is to be hoped that all here
present will have the opportunity to visit it.

John Bicknell was also the common ancestor of our family.
At the death of his father he was twelve years of age. Where
and how he lived during the remainder of his minority we do not
know, but we infer that he had such opportunities for education as
the country afforded; and as his occupation was that of a carpenter, it is probable at a suitable age he was apprenticed to the
seven years' service according to the customs of the time.

I find no record of his first marriage, but learn that his wife's
name was Mary, by the record of the births of his children. His
marriage would seem to have taken place about the year 1650,
when he was twenty-six years old. They had three children. Mary,
who married John Dyer, John[3] and Naomi. Mary, his wife, died
in 1658, March 25, and he married another Mary, the daughter of
Richard Porter of Weymouth,— an excellent genealogy of whose
family has been compiled and recently published by a descendant,
the Hon. J. W. Porter, of Burlington, Me.

The children by this second marriage were eight, three sons and
five daughters, making the whole number of his children eleven,
Ruth[3] married James Richards and Mary[3] married Maurice
Trufant. Of the other daughters there appears to be no recorded
account of either marriage or death.

John Bicknell died probably the last of the year 1678, as his
will is dated November 6, 1678, and allowed January 20, 1679.
In this will he names his wife Mary, and his son John[3] to be
executors. He gives all his estate to his wife (except twenty acres
and one and one-half acres of salt meadow which he gives to his
son John) so long as she shall remain his widow, to bring up the
children to the age of twenty-one.*

He gives to his daughters £15 each and to the three children of
John Dyer, viz: John Dyer, Thomas Dyer and Benjamin Dyer
£5 each, being his grandchildren.

From the evidence we now have, it would seem that John Bicknell's homestead was that now owned and occupied by a descend-

---

* He mentions no child by name except John 3.

ant, Thomas Bicknell. It is situated on Sea street near the
corner of Bridge street. It was the homestead of his son John[3],
and after his death it was conveyed by John[1], Zachariah[1] and
Ebenezer[1], sons of John[3] to their brother Benjamin[1], from whom
it has come in the direct line of descent to the present owner.

John Bicknell[3] died at the early age of fifty-four years, just after
filling the responsible and honorable office of representative for the
town of Weymouth, to the house of deputies of the Massachusetts
Bay Colony.

By inheritance, industry and prudence he seems to have acquired
a considerable estate, and by his good character, the confidence
and esteem of his fellow-citizens. We have no details of particular actions or deeds by which we can form our opinions of his
worth, but can only judge him by the work done by the community of which he was a part, and by whom he was found worthy
of confidence and trust.

The period of his life covered the years of the formation of our
most important institutions, and as we recede from that time our
wonder grows that our forefathers were gifted with the knowledge
and prudence demanded by the occasion.

A glance at a few of these questions may serve to refresh our
minds with the character of their work, and enable us the better
to appreciate it. Among the earlier measures requiring action
were the enlargement of their company by the admission of members and determining a rule of qualification for such membership.
The institution of the representative system when the plantations
had become so many as to make meetings of the whole body of
freemen for the transaction of business inconvenient. The formation of two distinct bodies in the government — the magistrates
and the deputies — with their separate and concurrent powers.
The powers and privileges which the people themselves in their
several local plantations should have and enjoy, both in secular
and ecclesiastical affairs. The granting of the lands among propri-
etors with incorporated powers and the tenure by which these
lands should be held by the individual members, the mode of con-
veyance and the laws of descent,— all of these questions came up
to be wrought by thought and agitation into their proper place, in
their system of government. That the consideration of these and
other important questions was attended with much difference of
opinion and that the discussion or " agitating of the question," as

our fathers were pleased to term it, gave rise to much warmth of feeling and sometimes to seeming harshness of action,— we have only to recur to the banishment of Roger Williams,— the great Antinomian controversy and the consequent banishment of Mrs. Hutchinson and Mr. Wheelwright and others ;—and even the training field in the neighboring town of Hingham, has become memorable in history as the scene of the earliest rebellion,—and as the occasion of " agitating " the proper bounds of the authority of the magistrates and the liberty of the people.

Of John Bicknell's three sons, John[3] the eldest lived and died in Weymouth. He had five sons and two daughters. One of the sons, Joseph, died at the early age of twenty years. Mary married John Turner of Bridgewater, and Sarah married William Sargent.

Zachary[3] married Hannah Smith in 1692. They had six children, four sons and two daughters. Five of these were born in Weymouth and the remaining son was born, probably, in that part of Swansea afterwards known as Barrington, Rhode Island, where his father removed about the year 1704.

Thomas[3] married Ann Turner in 1697. He removed from Weymouth to Pembroke or Middleborough, Mass. He seems to have been a blacksmith by trade. He died at Middleborough, Mass., February 17, 1718, at the age of forty-seven. I find no record of the births of his children and only know of them through the Probate Records of the settlement of his estate. They are Mary[4], Japhet[4], Hannah[4], and Elizabeth[4].

Thus by the emigration of Zachary[3] and Thomas[3] from Weymouth, the descendants of Zachary became separated, and in the lapse of time, their descendants lost knowledge of the relationship existing among them, except such as a faulty tradition had preserved.

The ever prolific source of the origin of so many of the families of New England that tradition loves to indulge in, the three brothers who came from England or some other country of Europe and settled in different parts of the country, would have some foundation could we commence with the third generation of our own family. The efforts made to follow out the several lines of descent from these three brothers to the sixth and seventh generations have been, in the line of the male members, more successful than could have been anticipated in the short time devoted to the work. The interest now manifested and of which this gathering is an earnest of still increased interest should enable us to accomplish more in the future, and we hope to see the chain complete, every link in its proper place.

As there were others at the early settlement of New England who bore the name of Bicknell, we shall undoubtedly meet with some who now bear the name, who do not belong to our family. We find in the Boston and Charlestown records the names of Edward, John and Samuel Bicknell, and we find also that the recording clerk has taken large liberties in various spellings of the name. I have found nothing to show any relationship between the Bicknells of Boston and Charlestown, and Zachary of Weymouth, and it is a little singular that most of those now bearing the family name so far as we meet with them, can trace their descent from Zachary of Weymouth. The descendants of Zachary have almost invariably in their own spelling of the name preserved the original and the correct form.

There were other Bicknells, some of whom settled at the Barbadoes, and in an account of that island, the names of several with their possessions are given, including bound servants and slaves; and in 1680 William Bicknell appears as an inhabitant of St. Michaels as having one servant and two slaves.

But few of the descendants of Zachary Bicknell reached the dignity of slave-owners, and these it will be found on an examination of their wills to have carefully regarded and tenderly cared for their slaves. On their manumission these former slaves so much respected the memories of their masters that they took the family name and their descendants are to be found to this day in some of our cities, bearing the name. This should be borne in mind that in looking for some honorable line of descent we may not go on a useless search to Africa. It would have added much to the interest of the occasion could some representatives of this branch of the family been present. This brief statement of history and fact is made to show the condition under which our ancestors were placed that we may the better appreciate their characters and labors.

They found their place, not among the scholars and learned men of the land, but in the more common industrial pursuits incident to a new country. That they performed their duties with an intelligent enterprise and success, their general comfortable condition

3

in life through so many generations bears evidence. Though none
of them became wealthy, yet all generally secured what was a
competency for the times in which they lived. They gave their
children the advantages the schools afforded and I have not met
with an instance where any of them were so deficient in the
common rudiments of education as to be unable to write their names.
They have generally been found among the conservative supporters of the institutions of religion from the time John Bicknell[2]
repaired the meeting-house to the present time, when the meet-
ing-houses of our land are filled with the learning and eloquence
of their descendants.

If the name in the earlier generations is found but seldom
among the legislators and magistrates of the land, it is believed
that the ability and integrity with which these positions have been
filled in later times show what the latent force of the name is equal
to, when brought into action in this direction.

In view of the honorable record of the past may we not congrat-
ulate ourselves, in this our first re-union, upon so worthy a record,
and should we not feel pressing upon us the obligation to preserve
and perpetuate the name unimpaired to those who shall follow us,
so revering the Puritan as to imitate his thought, of living always
in the divine presence and following the footsteps, with him, of
the Divine Master as we may understand his doctrine and example.

The following is a brief account of the male descendants of
Zachary Bicknell to the sixth generation. In some of the lines it
is not complete.

ZACHARY BICKNELL[1], 1590.

JOHN[2], 1624.

JOHN[3], 1653–4.	ZACHARIAH[3], 1667–8.	THOMAS[3], 1670.
John[4], 1688.	Zachariah[4], 1695.	Japhet[4].
Zachariah[4], 1691.	Joshua[4], 1696.	
Benjamin[4], 1694.	James[4], 1702.	
Joseph[4], 1698–9, d.	Peter[4], 1705 or 6.	
Ebenezer[4], 1700.		

JOHN[4].

John[5], 1715.	Joseph[5], 1719.	Nathaniel[5], 1725.

ZACHARIAH[4].

Zachariah[5], 1728.　Ezra[5], 1731, d.　David[5], 1734.　Lemuel[5], 1739.

BENJAMIN[4].

Benjamin[5], 1727

EBENEZER[4].

Ebenezer[5], 1727.
James[5], 1732, d.

ZACHARIAH[4].

Zachariah[5], 1723. John[5], 1725. Samuel[5], 1729.
Ebenezer[5] 1732. Timothy[5] 1733. William[5] 1735. Nathan[5] 1736-7.

JOSHUA[4].

Joshua[5], 1723. Allen[5], 1713, d.

JAMES[4].

James[5]. Moses[5].

PETER[4].

Peter[5], 1736, d. Peter[5], 1745. Asa[5], 1747. Amos[5].

JAPHET[4].

Japhet[5], 1750. Thomas[5], 1748-9. Turner[5], 1752.

JOHN[5].

John[6], 1744. Thomas[6], 1748. Jacob[6], 1751.

JOSEPH[5].

Joseph[6], 1751. Daniel[6], 1761. James[6], d.

NATHANIEL[5].

Luke[6], 1749. Nathaniel[6], 1756. Humphrey[6], 1762. Otis[6], 1764.

ZACHARIAH[5].

Ezra[6], 1753. Stephen[6], 1751, d. Zachariah[6], 1756. Peter[6], 1759.

DAVID[5].

Samuel[6], 1757. Levi[6], 1759. David[6], 1771, d. Elijah[6], 1773, d.
David[6], 1776. Elijah[6], 1777.

LEMUEL[5].

Abner[6], 1764. Lemuel[6], 1770. John[6], 1779.

Benjamin[5].

Benjamin[6], 1748, d. Benjamin[6], 1770, d. Peter[6], 1774.
Thomas[6], 1780. Benjamin[6], 1786.

Ebenezer[5].

James[6], 1758.

Zachariah[5], No ch. John[5], No ch.

Samuel[5].

Samuel[6], 1773. David[6], 1775, d.

Ebenezer[5].

Josiah[6], 1760. Ephraim[6], 1769. Benjamin[6], 1773.

Timothy[5], No ch.

William[5].

Zachariah[6], 1760. Timothy[6], 1767. William[6], 1777.

Nathan[5].

Elijah[6], 1765. Nathaniel[6], 1768. Isaac[6], 1770. Nathan[6], 1774.

Joshua[5].

Thomas[6], 1747. James[6], 1749. Joshua[6], 1759.
Winchester[6], 1761, d. Joseph[6], 1763.

Moses[5].

James[6], 1764. Calvin[6]. Bennet[6]. Daniel[6].

Peter[5].

Peter[6], 1770. Kent[6], 1771. John Payn[6], 1780. Hezekiah[6], 1785.

Asa[5].

Asa[6], 1771, d. Otis[6], 1773, d. John Wilson[6], 1780.
William[6] 1782. Benjamin Ellery[6] 1786. Asa[6] 1788. Francis[6] 1793.

Japhet[5].

Jesse[6], 1770. Japhet[6], 1772.

Thomas[5].

Thomas W. T.[6] George Augustus[6], 1787. Daniel Dexter[6].

HISTORICAL ADDRESS.

BY GEORGE A. BICKNELL.

E are told that America is the oldest of the continents; that being first fit for human habitation, it was first inhabited by races long ago extinct. We are told also that the physical influences of this country have been fatal to every race that has occupied it; that as a people, we ourselves are degenerating, losing our productive vigor, and that without continued accessions of new blood from abroad, we should speedily wear out and pass away, like the races which have preceded us " in this new world which is the old."

But this gathering suggests that one family, at least, has not shared in this alleged universal degeneracy, but exhibits to-day, after the lapse of eight generations, as much physical vigor, as much sound sense, and as much moral force as belonged to its representatives, two hundred and fifty years ago.

Christianity teaches that all mankind are descended from a single pair, yet the philosophers assert that certain regions produce distinct forms of animal and vegetable life, not found elsewhere, and they say that distinct races of men flourish in peculiar districts, indigenous there, and capable of prevailing there in the great struggle for existence, so that, as far as human records or human traditions go, the white, the yellow, the black and the red races have always occupied in force their own climates and have made no thorough development elsewhere.

Whatever may be true as to the origin of man and his diverse races, it cannot be denied that all the conquests and migrations and interminglings of nations have hitherto failed to produce a new race of men.

The teaching of History is that Nature abhors a mongrel; a nation of mulattoes is an impossibility, for whenever different races are compelled in violation of their natural instincts, to dwell together in large bodies, whether on terms of legal and social equality, or otherwise, one of them invariably destroys or absorbs the others, so that all the distinctive features of the latter are at last completely obliterated.

In this country we have destroyed the red man, we shall destroy or absorb the black man.

In England, the Norman and the Saxon could readily mingle; they were varieties of the same stock; but the Englishman of to-day is not the Englishman of Cressy and Poictiers: the England of to-day is not the England of Cromwell or of Pitt; the Norman type is wearing out, the more numerous Saxon is prevailing; the Norman pluck and vigor which leavened the heavy Saxon masses and made England the arbitress of Europe for centuries, are gone, and the old glory of England has gone with them.

The Normans were the highest type of manhood that Europe ever saw. Less intellectual than the Greeks, more intellectual than the Romans, superior to both in physical endurance, in personal prowess, and in practical achievements with small means, the blood of that band of heroes runs in the veins of every monarchy in Europe. That Norman blood, my kinsmen and kinswomen, is our blood.

This country has been chiefly settled by the best varieties of the white races. The great Scandinavian or Teutonic and the Celtic families are kindred stock; the Latin nations of Europe which in a less degree have contributed to our population are also, more remotely, our kinsmen; undoubtedly, one of these types will predominate here, and will absorb the others; then, and not until then, shall we be a homogeneous people; then, and not until then, shall we produce in this country, that purely American literature and

American poetry and American art, of which hitherto we have had
only feeble premonitions.

I believe that individual greatness arises commonly in blood to
a certain extent homogeneous. The ancestors of Franklin for many
generations were small mechanics in a remote English village; in
such a community, by frequent inter-marriages, the whole population, at length, becomes akin, and the blood, thus becoming to a
certain extent homogeneous, it is presently illustrated, by a great
man.

So it was with Lord Thurlow and with Sir Walter Scott, they
both inherited homogeneous blood; they and Franklin were all great,
in their different lines, but they all married out of the charmed circle,
and their greatness died with them, "no son of theirs succeeding."
Although the maxim, "Like produces like," has its exceptions,
it is not less true of mankind than of other animals, and that
maxim is the foundation of all such gatherings as this; the presump-
tion is that the common ancestor has transmitted to all of us
something of the same kind, and that something is the common
bond of union and equality among us; without it, the descendants
of Zachary Bicknell would be no more to us, than the descendants
of any body else.

This power of transmitting to remote descendants peculiar traits
of form and feature and temperament and moral character, thus
reproducing indefinitely your own body and your own soul, is one
of the wonders of physiology.

We know that every man has ancestors innumerable; we know
that, if for twenty preceding generations, none of our lineal ancestors were consanguineous, each of us would have at the distance
of twenty generations, more than a million of ancestors, to wit,
two parents, four grandparents, eight great-grandparents, and so
on, in rapidly increasing progression.

Yet, notwithstanding this union of so many strains of blood, we
often behold one of them predominating over all the others, and
impressing its own peculiarities upon generation after generation
as long as the family endures.

We all remember the thick lip of the House of Austria and the
peculiar physiognomy of the Bourbons, and we know that in an
adjacent State, where a bad woman was confined in jail for crime,
two hundred of her descendants, in the course of a few generations, were the inmates of the State's prison or the jail.

I know the corrective power of education, but it is a limited power; when "the fathers have eaten sour grapes the children's teeth are set on edge:" no training will "gather grapes from thorns or figs from thistles."

I say this power of hereditary transmission is one of the world's wonders; it is the foundation of all family pride and family self-respect, it is a potent incentive to virtuous conduct: without it, it would be entirely immaterial whether we have a long line of honorable ancestry, or whether

> "Our ancient but ignoble blood
> Has crept through scoundrels ever since the flood,"

Our ancestor Zachary Bicknell came here in 1635. He came with a band of Puritans who brought their church and their minister. What they sought in this wilderness was freedom to worship God! They were not deluded by dreams of empire; they were not stimulated by the feverish excitement of mercantile adventure; they were following none of the phantoms of pleasure; they were plain, earnest, God-fearing men; they came to plant their church in the desert, that "the wilderness and the solitary place might be glad for them." This place of their settlement then bore its Indian name of Wessagussett: it had been settled before under less favorable conditions, that settlement had melted away, the ground was vacant again, our colony took it and flourished and has never ceased to flourish.

It has sent out swarm after swarm of hardy emigrants, until the descendants of the first settlers of Wessaguscus, now called Weymouth, are found everywhere, from Maine to Georgia and from the Atlantic to the Pacific.

In the list of that colony our ancestors are thus recorded: "Zachary Bicknell, aged 45; Agnes, his wife, aged 27; John, his son, aged 11, and John Kitchin, his servant, aged 23." This is the entire record.

Twenty acres of ground were assigned to him as a place for his mansion; he built it in Middle street; we shall visit its site to-day.

His English home was near Weymouth, in Dorsetshire, on the southern coast of England, a place noted for salubrity in the old Roman times.

Accustomed to ease and comfort, in that wild region he soon yielded to the rigor of our harsh climate and to the hardships of a new settlement, and he died in 1637, at the early age of forty-seven years.

There is a tradition in my branch of the family, that he was a captain in the British Navy, retired on half pay, but his title in the colony was Zachary Bicknell, gentleman. He left a competent fortune to his only son, John, who became one of the solid men of Weymouth, but he, too, died young; the family had not yet become acclimated, yet it was beginning to reassert its vigor. John had three sons and seven daughters, and from these three grandsons of the original settler, all who bear our name in this country are believed to be descended. The names of these grandsons were John and Zachary and Thomas. The descendants of John, the first grandson, remained, generally, in Weymouth, where, I am told, they number now about twenty voters.

The descendants of Zachary, the second grandson, migrated first to Barrington and thence to Mansfield and to Ashford in Connecticut, and their representatives may be found in Vermont, Massachusetts, New York, Wisconsin, Kentucky and on the Pacific coast.

The descendants of Thomas, the third grandson, settled in Attleboro, where they remained for several generations, but within the present century they have found homes in Pennsylvania, New York, Indiana, Iowa, Texas and California.

Since its acclimation in this country our family has been vigorous, healthy, long-lived and prolific.

We have not taken a very active part in public affairs.

John, the son of the first settler, was a member of the Legislature of Massachusetts. In the line of John, the first grandson, we find several members of the Legislature; and in the line of Zachary, the second grandson, we find a Judge of the Supreme Court of Rhode Island, and a member of Congress from New York.

In the line of Thomas, the third grandson, we find a Circuit Judge of Indiana, a member of Congress from Indiana, a lieutenant in the U. S. Navy, and the rector of an Episcopal church.

We have had several clergymen among us, some merchants and manufacturers, many mechanics, very few lawyers, no doctors that I know of, and, I believe, none of those wily intriguers sometimes called politicians.

Prior to 1824, the Bicknells were generally Federalists, since then they have not commonly acted with the Democrats.

Until the beginning of the present century the principal representatives of the family were engaged almost exclusively in agriculture.

> " Along the cool, sequestered vale of life
> They kept the noiseless tenor of their way."

Hence our virtues, our faults and our eccentricities have been those of a rural people—independent owners of the soil. Accustomed for generations to the seclusion of the farm, we have been somewhat exclusive in our associations; having been much alone for generations, we have become secretive and reticent, with too little regard, perhaps, for public opinion, or the opinions of others; used to the absolute rule of our own farms, we have become impatient of opposition.

Such a people have few temptations to crime. Their freedom from temptation coupled with favorable tendencies in the blood, and aided by favorable moral surroundings under Puritan influences, has produced one remarkable result. I allude to the absence of crime in the annals of this family since its settlement in America. Our American genealogy covers nine or ten generations, including the first settler, yet, it is asserted by those who claim to know, that in the last two hundred and fifty years, not one of the blood of Zachary Bicknell, bearing his surname has ever stood convicted in any court, of any crime, or misdemeanor, or fraud. If this be so, we have the noblest of all pedigrees.

But who was Zachary Bicknell? Whence did he come? What were his antecedents?

Undoubtedly he was of Scandinavian origin. He belonged to that great northern stock which regenerated the stagnation of the Middle Ages, and gave tone to the civilization of modern Europe.

His name is Swedish. The name Becknill in Swedish is equivalent to Brookhill in English; it was the name of the spot occupied by the family and with which they became identified.

I know of no records giving the date of the migration from that ancient seat to the British Islands, but there is a tradition in my branch of the family, that long ago, before the introduction of Christianity into Britain, and while the country north and south of the Tweed for many miles was an independent heathen kingdom, our ancestor brought his forces in ships and landed north of the Tweed, in what is now southeastern Scotland, and there maintained himself by force of arms until he was recognized as a vassal by the ruler of the kingdom. The story goes that, the site of the stronghold he occupied there took the name afterwards of Bicknell hill and still retains that name, and that from that spot the family dispersed itself throughout England and into Ireland and Wales. This is only a tradition, it may go for its worth, but the name is conclusive evidence of Scandinavian origin.

It was changed in Great Britain from Becknill to Bicknell; it has maintained the latter form with great persistency, has undergone some variations; here in Weymouth, many years ago, one of the family wrote his name Bucknell; in Barrington some of the descendants of the second grandson called themselves Bicknall; in England there have been other corruptions, such as Bucknill, Bucknall, Buckner, Bicknor, Bignall, Bagnall and Bagenal.

Sometimes such changes occur when the offshoots of a family sink into ignorance; sometimes they are due to the different dialects of different parts of England; sometimes, like the changes made by our Weymouth and Barrington kinsmen, they are purely whimsical.

Mental peculiarities of families may be often traced to the influence of laws and customs prevailing at a very remote period among the races to which they belong.

Certain social institutions of the early northern nations of Europe are reflected in opinions and feelings which have been inherent in our family in all its vicissitudes and which are still in force among us, although they are contrary to the leading thought of this country, and cannot be logically defended.

I allude to the general impression amongst us that we belong to a superior stock. Since we have been in this country we have never had extravagant wealth, we have never exercised great power, we have never sought public distinction, yet I have never met one of the name, high or low, rich or poor, enlightened or ignorant, who was not persuaded that he had an inheritance as one of us, more precious than rubies.

I find the origin of this feeling in the twilight of history. It is not the growth of this country, nor of its institutions. But, among our Scandinavian ancestors, there was a clear legal distinction, so old that its beginning can not be traced, between the man who was merely free, and the man who was not only free but also noble.

They had three classes only of society, the earl, who was gentle, the churl, who was simple, and the thrall, who was a slave.

The earl, born gentle, seems to have had, originally, no peculiar privileges, certainly no oppressive ones, but he was entitled by his blood to special respect and honor, which the churl, born simple, might win, but never inherited.

These distinctions were the essential elements of primeval Teutonic Society; they were so ground into its framework, that the early legends represented the three classes, the earl, the churl, and the thrall, as the separate creations of the gods.

I apprehend that this shadowy claim of ours to some special advantage that cannot be defined by ourselves, nor recognized by our neighbors, is the result of these ancient institutions, operating still after the lapse of ages; its existence shows the power and permanence of ideas, accepted and grafted into the heart of a people. It is the dim traditional remembrance of an ancient worth, which we would fain hope may be perpetual.

When our ancestors landed at Wessagussett, Charles the first of England was preparing the way for the long Parliament and the Revolution; the thirty years' war was raging on the continent of Europe; Gustavus Adolphus had lately fallen at Lützen; Cardinal Richelieu was ruling the destinies of France; the age of Cromwell and Mazarin and Louis the fourteenth was yet to come.

In this country, the entire possessions of England were a few scanty and scattered settlements along the Atlantic; the Spaniards had St. Augustine, the Dutch had the island of Manhattan; the Swedes had not yet made their settlement on the Delaware.

Our people are now nearly fifty millions. We are the only truly grand Republic that the world ever saw; we have filled the American continent, from Canada to Mexico, and from ocean to ocean with a hardy, industrious, intelligent and Christian people.

At first glance it would seem that all the essential advancement of humanity in the useful arts and inventions, in science, in manufactures, in the general diffusion of knowledge, in the recognition of human rights and in the establishment of civil liberty, has been accomplished in the last two hundred and fifty years.

Perhaps no other equal period of time has exhibited such amazing results.

And here the question arises, have we as a family borne our part in this great progression? If not, we have been false to ourselves, and unworthy of our descent. If not, let us do more hereafter; if we can do little ourselves, let us give to our issue such moral training and education as may help them to do more; for we may be sure that without some practical demonstration of excellence, all our pride in our ancestry will be but "as sounding brass or tinkling cymbals."

The lineal descendants of the celebrated Confucius are living now in China, exercising honorable offices of public trust; their ancestors, for seventy successive generations, have illustrated the enduring excellence of that strain of blood; their essential nobility has survived all the chances and the changes of more than twenty centuries.

No such examples are possible in this western world; it is the design of our institutions to exalt the body-politic, and not to exalt individual families.

In this country acquired honors are not inherited; death scatters accumulated wealth; families, commonly, fade away and are forgotten in a few generations; the exceptions that are permanent enjoy rare physical vigor and distinguished purity of morals.

We, as a family, number ten generations here, eight of them American born; few of us may attain the factitious respectability that goes with large possessions; few of us may enjoy the distinction of public honors; but every one of us can maintain and is bound to maintain the ancient honor, the upright integrity, and the sound morality of this family; these are our best inheritance, let us transmit them unimpaired and brightened to those who shall follow us. Let us remember that

> "Only the ashes of the just
> Smell sweet and blossom in the dust."

Let us remember that

> "One sad losel soils a name for aye
> However glorious in the olden time;
> Not all that heralds rake from coffin'd clay
> Nor florid prose, nor honeyed words in rhyme
> Can blazon of evil deeds, or consecrate a crime."

If such be our ruling spirit, then when another hundred years shall have passed away and the Bicknells of future generations shall meet, on this consecrated spot of their American origin, to unroll the record of the past, and revive ancestral memories, they shall be more exalted than we, and shall illustrate with more honor the ancient worth of the race.

The following hymn was sung at the close of the exercises in the church, before adjournment for dinner :

FAMILY HYMN.

September 22, 1880.

BY ALFRED BICKNELL, MELROSE, MASS.

Tune—AMERICA.

I.

Joyful we gather here,
With brimming hearts to cheer,
  Each kinsman new.
From north and south and west,
Grateful for favors blest,
We come, in loving quest,
  This scene to view,—

II.

Our family, returned
To this old home, where burned
  The earliest fire,
Which, on this northern strand
To warm their Pilgrim band,
Was kindled by the hand
  Of our GRANDSIRE.

III.

That warmth can ne'er depart
From any loyal heart
  That owns our name.

Unquenched by time or space,
By Heaven's sustaining grace,
In every age and place,
  It burns the same.

IV.

When Christmas time is near,
We seek the homes so dear,
  At Love's glad call,—
So, on this autumn day,
The summons we obey,
And come in full array,
  Each greeting all.

V.

Right welcome to this place!
Welcome each cousin's face,
  Fruit of our tree!
Hail to each new-found friend!
May Heaven its bounty lend,
And may success attend
  Our JUBILEE!

A Bicknell Idyl.

BY MRS. ACHSA H. (BICKNELL) AMES, COLUMBIA, PENN.

DEAR Friends and Kindred— far away,
I give you greeting—all to-day—
Each friendly hand I fain would grasp
In a long, thrilling, loving clasp.
But seas of circumstance divide,
As sure as ocean's rolling tide.
And what I have to say or think,
Must go to you by pen and ink.
Fate dooms my vision may not see
This old new-gathered family ;
My willing feet no road may trace
To your time-honored meeting place.
So at this BICKNELL Jubilee
Another will my proxy be,—
Linking—Dear Cousins—you and me.

" Lang syne " my feet have trod the street
In the old town where you will meet ;
And memory dear around it weaves
A charm,—bright as its autumn leaves ;
My Mother's Birthplace! Shall I not
Do reverence to this hallowed spot?

As from the hill top, gained at last,
Over the way we came,— we cast
Our eyes with long drawn earnest gaze
At the far landscape,— lost in haze,
So we, though veiled in distance blue,
The journey of our sires review.

Long — long ago,— one summer's day
The waves of Massachusetts Bay
Were parted by the oaken prow
Of the " Assurance;" freighted now
With stern souls from " Old England " come
To found in this " New World" a home.
On deck more than a hundred stand;
The seed corn for this virgin land.
From " Weymouth " old, for " Weymouth " new,
Sires, dames and babes; a royal crew,
Fit followers of that Plymouth stock
Late planted on the world-famed " Rock."

ZACHARY,— AGNES,— JOHN ! Over their biers
The winds have blown two hundred years.
But as the breezes come and go
In all the ages man shall know,
May their blest memory sacred be
Who planted here the BICKNELL tree;
Their " Requiem " the sounding sea.

As in the spring the well tilled field
Gives promise of autumnal yield:—
So in those spring-time days of yore,
Our tree paternal fruitage bore
In numbers rich.   Each branching shoot
In new homes added to the fruit
Already ripening;— till the town
Itself too small for them was found :
South, West and North they emigrate,
A welcome find in many a State.
More homes they plant throughout the Nation
And quite outgrow all calculation.

At this late day we cannot tell
The old, old story. passing well;
For little record has been left
By which to trace the warp and weft
Of all the yards wove, since the day
Our Fathers entered this broad bay :—
By History's shuttle : flying fast
· As it e'er must while time shall last.
But a few words,— mere feeble hints
Of what has happened to us, since
The household " parting of the ways "
(Leading asunder like the rays
Of bounteous light.— and like that too
As wider thrown, more good to do).

Near to this spot that farmhouse stood
From which departed the young blood
Fortunes to seek.   And now again
After so long,— back to " Old Spain "
We come, as pilgrims to their shrines ;
Or children to their homes returning,
Their hearts for household faces yearning,
Glad each new cousin now to know ;
Uniting here the parted lines
Sundered so many years ago.

The oldest,— John,— at home remained ;
And age of manhood having gained,
As was quite proper,— took a wife ;
And lived a sober, quiet life
For many years ; his duty doing
To all around ; no myths pursuing,
But practical, and steady going.
And now the fruit of this good sowing
Is seen in many a household here,
On all the hillsides far and near.
For specimen wheat if you desire
Say our " Toast Master "— Zachariah !

4

The second southward took his way
(Named for " Grandfather Zach."— they say),
And by the " Narragansetts " bay
Sees. what appears to his glad eyes,
Place for a farm of goodly size!
The soil was fair, and as they grew
The " boys" could have a farm there, too.
These waters, too; nice place for fish;
And clams! so many that no dish
Could cook them right;— so in the ground
Dug caves; the only way they found!!
But in this world surprises come.
He found what seemed a fair-sized home
Was more! in fact, strange to relate,
The whole of " Little Rhody's " State!
This, they, of course, soon overflow,
And westward the grandchildren go.
Some in the " Empire State " remain,
Some. pushing on, " Ohio " gain.
I will not vouch that all is true
Of these details, as told to you.
I cannot.— for I was not there
To see; but cousin Thomas, in the chair
Is of that branch: and sure he " oughter "
Know if the story will " hold water."
Young Thomas, too, picked up his bundle;
Thinking it time for him to trundle
His worldly gear; and as its wings
The young bird tries before it springs
For higher flights,— he started out
For a short trip,— finding, no doubt
His wish; for in a neighboring borough
Where land was good he turned a furrow
Hard by the State, where, as you know,
The well-known " wooden nutmegs " grow.
And well they delved, no labor shirking
When, wishing for new fields to work in
Some left New England, and their banner
Planted upon the Susquehanna.
Where Penn, so famed in song and story,

Founded the city,—now his glory.
But still the children will not stay
Under their roof tree,— and away
Some go to the " far, far West;"
To those broad acres, where the best
Of crops are gathered,— wheat and corn
And children,— good as ever born!
Of fruit from that branch of our tree.
If you are curious now to see,
I name (*sub rosa*) our " M. C."

And so they " live and thrive and grow "
Until our day, and here, we show
These samples of that Pilgrim blood,
That crossed old ocean's stormy flood
With Zachary and his manly boy.
May future Bicknells feel like joy,
And show results as sound and true
As have come down from them to you.
Pardon me, cousins, if I stray
From themes of larger scope to-day,
And read to you a single leaf
Of personal history. 'Tis, in brief,
Like many another, which you all
In your ancestors' lives recall.
'Tis but one stone uncarved and rude
In this Fane, pillared with our blood.
A single note in the grand song
That to our name and land belong.
Let me bring back that olden time
(Whose memory stirs like vesper chime
Stealing across some shadowed bay
Pearl-tinted by the dying day) :
When, childhood's busy labor done,
I sat me down at set of sun
To hear the story told again
Of a long journey down to " Maine ! "
Of Grandpa Noah, so strong and bold,
And his wife, Nancy, good as gold.
Of Emery, the first-born son.

And Hannah, daughter number one;
Of James, a little toddling fellow,
And baby Nancy, on a pillow.
How, for a farmer's life inclined,
They left old Weymouth's hills behind,
And in a wagon roofed with white,
In which the children took delight,
They journeyed on through bush and brake,
By winding stream and woodland lake,
Onward, towards the rising sun,
Until the tiresome journey done.
Noah's "ark of safety" victory won,
Until their "Ararat" they found
Where Oxford's dark, old woods abound.
As time rolled on more children came
To propagate the Bicknell name.
One daughter and three lusty boys
Filling the new-made home with noise.
And then a grandchild, who in time
Grew fond of scribbling prose and rhyme,
Who, here and now, would fain rehearse
This old time tale in better verse.
Of other branches and their fruit
The past, to me, is sadly mute.
But all will represented be,
I trust, on our ancestral tree.
And your Historian deftly trace
Each branch and scion to its place.
Your "President" we know by sight,
His "Journal" bringing us delight.
Toilers in the same field are we,—
Abundant may the harvest be,—
Not gauged by gold, or worldly store,
But rich in words and works of Power
To help to higher, nobler life
The youth now arming for the strife
Of the world's battle. So shall we
Gain by our giving; and at last,
When all this mortal toil is past,
And we shall cross the narrow sea,

May we in loving, joyous bands,
Meet the warm clasp of welcoming hands.

Not far away from where I write,
Enrobed in pure, immortal white
A sculptured CLIO sits.   Around
Her snowy feet 'tis hallowed ground,
Where our good LINCOLN bared his head
To eulogize the Nation's Dead!
Fair fields of Gettysburg; one line
In memory of thee and thine.
Could I invoke her magic power,
And wield her marble pen one hour,
These lines should thrill your listening ears,
Should fill your answering eyes with tears,
Strengthen your inmost souls, for fight
Against the wrong, tho' armed with might.
Pledging anew each loyal soul
In Freedom's sacred army roll,
Allay all doubt,— dispel all fears —
And warm your hearts for coming years.

Sometimes the northern breeze brings down
A message to this German town;
Telling in accents soft and low
Of those I knew so long ago.
Bringing to our delighted ears
The story of successful years.
The brush one wields with rising fame;
One labors in his Master's name;
Some till the soil, some thrive at trade,
For arts mechanic some seem made;
But laggards, none! a drone alive
Is stranger to the Bicknell hive!
Sometimes we hear of bridal bells;
Or ringing laugh of baby glee
Chorus of sweetest melody!
And sometimes, sad funereal knells,
Telling that servants tried and true,
Faithful with many as with few,

Their sun low sinking in the west
Are summoned, "Enter into rest."
The latest carrier dove that flew
Straight to the Susquehanna's blue,
Brought down the welcome invitation
To meet this new " Association ! "
I wish that health and purse said " Yea,"
But Prudence, safer guide, says " Nay,
Be patient." So I send this greeting,
Hoping to be at your next meeting.
The circle widens, — another year
Will bring them all, from far and near.

Kinswomen, who have changed your names
(Not one, like me, I think, to Ames), '
I send you greeting. May this verse
Find you possessors of none worse.
And may each one of you have joy
Like me, in one, big Bicknell boy !
Please pardon, if I add a line
On lineage, of this son of mine,
(Altho' I hold the best of blood
Is that which keeps us doing good :—
And the best legacy that's given
Is manhood, and the hope of Heaven :
A little pride may pardoned be
Because of virtuous family).
When I of " Zachary " discourse,
His father names another source,
Old Fisher Ames ! the eloquent,
Once Harvard's chosen President.
And all agree that we should be
Honored by honest progeny.

My fair young cousins ; human flowers,
Adorning this gray band of ours,—
Upon the green and fragrant banks
Where bloom your sweet and scented ranks,
May one " wild oat " ne'er stay or drop
To propagate a sinful crop.

But in your sunshine's golden glow
May you to full perfection grow,
To guard the honor of our name,
Dearer by far than wealth or fame.

Let us rejoice :— no spendthrift son
Comes home in rags to ask a bone !
But as the rivers flowing free
Down to a common, glorious sea,
Come to this gathering old and young,
Those known to fame, and those not sung
In song or story ; but who yet,
Ere their life's sun shall sink and set,
By worthy word or labor done,
May carve their name on pillared stone.

What is the lesson heard to-day?
What does the voice historic say
To us,— as down the stream of Time
Comes many a message,— grand, sublime,
Feeble or foolish,— as the ears
That catch the accents read the years?
It speaks of homely duties done,
Of fields from native wildness won,—
Of thankless tasks performed with zeal,
Of works of mercy, and of weal
For those unable to repay :
Of tireless labor day by day
In years when plenty was unknown,
It points to many a happy home
(Not mansion grand, but cottage hearth),
Not station high, but modest worth,
It tells of Faith, and Hope, and Trust,
Showing that "treasure," that the " rust
And moth " of all the years
Dims not, but brighter yet appears.
It says " Fear not the right to do,"—
Warns us no folly to pursue,—
Strengthens the outstretched hand of Love,
By daily work our creed to prove ;

Sees Earth, as by His bounty given;
Our FATHER,— GOD! our home,—in Heaven.

Time tarries not :— my song must cease —
But ere we part.— I pray the " peace
That passeth all," — our lot may be
For time, and for Eternity.
'Tis fitting we should here rejoice
In these old new-found "girls" and "boys."
'Tis fitting that we join to cheer
Our gathered household, old and dear :
" Three cheers " for all who bear our name,
And three for all who love the same.
Three for old Zachary, and his sons.
Back to those five our blood all runs.
Three for this good old town, their home,
Good for a thousand years to come.
Three for each State that holds our kin.
Three for each Bicknell home within.
Three for our Brother, who fills the chair,
Three for our Statesman,— three for our " fair."
Three for our Artists, Lawyers, Teachers,
Three for our Farmers, and our Preachers,
Three for our Daughters, Wives and Mothers,
Three for our Fathers, Cousins, Brothers.
Three for our Flag, and " three times three "
For Law, for Love, for Liberty!

Time tarries not,— Dear friends, Good bye,
In the far space beyond the sky,
Some glorious world, we hope, may be
Our home throughout Eternity.
Hedged by no name, however bright :
Bounded by naught but Love and Right.
One common, perfect family,—
Our Father's children — all : may we
United be :— no parting sigh,—
Never again to say " GOOD BYE."

THE RE-UNION.

THE 22d of September was one of the brightest of our Autumn days. The clear and cool air, the bright sun, and the recent rains, made the day a perfect one for the gathering of the family at the old homestead, at Weymouth. The Committee of Arrangements in connection with the local committees had made complete preparation for the exercises. The Methodist Episcopal Church of East Weymouth, politely offered by the Trustees for the services, was admirably adapted as a place for the meeting. The Committee on flowers made ample and tasteful floral decorations. As early as 9.30 A. M., members of the family arrived at the church, and as the time for the commencement of the exercises drew near, the large audience room was well filled with the descendants of Zachary and Agnes Bicknell, each wearing a silk badge, commemorative of the occasion. Carriages and trains brought friends and relatives from far and near, (representing at least ten States of our country, with an honorable representative from the fatherland, England), and the introductions of the early hours of the day may help to form the acquaintanceships and friendships of a lifetime.

The church was tastefully decorated with tablets inscribed with the family Christian names of past generations, intermingled with beautiful flowers, the floral adornments including an elegant basket of tuberoses and other choice flowers. On the wall at each side of the altar were two tablets inscribed—"Old Weymouth welcomes the descendants of Zachary and Agnes Bicknell to their old home," and "1635—Zachary, Agnes, John, Mary, Thomas, John, Zachary.—Your children gather here to honor your memory.—1880."

The exercises were opened with an organ voluntary—the Grand Offertoire of Battiste—performed by Mr. Arthur M. Raymond, and the Arion Quartette then gave a vocal selection, "Welcome Meeting," by L. Marshall. The musical portion of the exercises was under the direction of F. B. Bates, Esq., and the choir was composed of musical talent of the family almost exclusively.

Rev. George W. Bicknell, of Lowell, chaplain of the day, read Scripture selections from the 25th chapter of Isaiah, and offered a fervent prayer, the choir stationed in the ante-room appropriately responding with a musical rendering of the Lord's Prayer.

Lest the elements of personality and family partiality should enter into our own account of the literary and musical exercises of the day we will refer our readers to the

NEWSPAPER REPORTS.

The *Weymouth Gazette* and *Weymouth Advance* in their issues of September 24. contained interesting and valuable reports of the Bicknell gathering, and the *Advance* published the President's address entire. As a remembrance of the Boston press, we print entire that of the *Boston Advertiser*, of Thursday, September 23.

THE BICKNELLS.

FIRST GATHERING AT EAST WEYMOUTH YESTERDAY OF THE FAMILY ASSOCIA-
TION — ADDRESS OF WELCOME — BRIEF FAMILY HISTORY — ADDRESS BY
CONGRESSMAN BICKNELL AND VISITS TO HISTORIC FAMILY SITES.

The Bicknells, one of our steady-going, conservative families,— the sort of stuff that makes New England stock respected everywhere, its morals strong and pure, and its industry thriving and solidly grounded,— held their first family re-union yesterday at East Weymouth. They have not as a family tended and watched the old family tree so closely that they can tell the exact connection between the blossoms and young boughs of to-day and the sturdy old parent stock. But as the tree is known by its fruits, therefore the fruits must show similarity to each other as well as to the original stock, and so there is abundant reason to expect that the effort to build up the family history, which was begun only a short time ago, will be successful to a satis-factory degree. The Bicknell Family Association was organized last Decem-ber. Its president is Mr. Thomas W. Bicknell of this city, the editor of the *New England Journal of Education;* the secretary and treasurer is Mr. Robert T. Bicknell of 200 Devonshire street, and the corresponding secretary is Mr. Alfred Bicknell of 33 Milk street. Yesterday the gathering was large and most encouraging to those who earnestly desire to keep trace of the family. Representatives from various parts of Massachusetts, near and remote, and from other States, came back to the old home of him to whom they trace their common descent, and who was one of the early pioneers in this New England wilderness. The Methodist Episcopal Church at East Weymouth was fittingly decorated for the day, and the audience of Bicknells and invited guests nearly filled it. From one of the pulpit side-lights hung the family coat-of-arms; flowers adorned the desk, and various placards showed the lines of patriarchs in the family. At the left of the pulpit was a large card bearing the inscription: " 1635. Zachary. Agnes, John, Mary, Thomas,

John, Zachary. Your children gather here to honor your memory. 1880."
A corresponding card on the other side read, " Old Weymouth welcomes the
descendants of Zachary and Agnes Bicknell to their old home." Down both
sides of the church, suspended from the wall-lights, were cards bearing well-
known family names, as follows: "William, Noah, James;" "Zachary,
John, Thomas;" "Luke, Humphrey, Otis;" "Timothy, Jacob, Ebenezer,
Daniel;" "Joseph, Benjamin, Nathan;" "Ezra, David, Samuel;" "Peter,
Joshua, Nathaniel;" "Joseph, Stephen, Allen." Music for the day was kindly
furnished by a volunteer choir of the family.

Eleven o'clock was the time set for the opening of the exercises, and the
first number was an organ voluntary. Then came reading of the Scriptures
and prayer by the Rev. George Bicknell of Lowell, who was the chaplain of
the day. A brief address of welcome was then given by Mr. Thomas W.
Bicknell, the president of the association. He mentioned the various branches
of the family and the leading family traits. While the family has not risen
to an exalted place, yet it has an honorable record. Many of its members
have been those who earned their bread by the sweat of their brows. Yet
they have a record which few families can show. For two hundred years of
which they have a record, not a member of the family has been a pauper or
a criminal. A good history has been made in the legislative halls of the
country. Several members of the family have been members of State legis-
latures, and two of them have been members of Congress. Among the family
there have been also business men, lawyers and a few doctors. The speaker
welcomed the guests and members of the family to the town of their common
ancestor and gave them a cordial greeting. After him came Mr. Quincy
Bicknell of Hingham, the historian of the association. His record involved
much patient search and care in arrangement, albeit when finished it sounded,
as one of his auditors remarked, like one of the chapters in the Bible which
are composed mainly of a series of " begat " sandwiches. After alluding to
the circumstances of the early immigration to Massachusetts and the character
of the immigrants, Mr. Bicknell spoke of the first one of the name in the
country,—Zachary Bicknell, who came to Weymouth in 1635. It can be
fairly inferred, said the speaker, although but little is known of Zachary,
that he was in sympathy with the early Puritan spirit, and that he was a man
of some property, for it is on record that he brought a servant with him.
Zachary died the year after his arrival, and the land in Weymouth which he
owned was sold in the next year to William Reed. In that family it remained
many years, and a person is now living who can remember when the last
Reed owner held it, so that its connection with the old Zachary is well established. The land is on Middle street and is the estate of the late Sylvanus
Bates. John Bicknell, son of Zachary, was also the common ancestor of all
the Bicknells in the country. He was twelve years old at the death of his
father, and grew up to be a carpenter. From this point the speaker went on
at length to speak of John's two marriages and eleven children. They became
widely dispersed, going to Maine, western Massachusetts and elsewhere, and
the success which has already been achieved in tracing the families warrants
the expectation that the record will be made still more complete. Other

Bicknells are found in the Boston and Charlestown records, but they do not seem to belong to this family, which includes most persons of the name in the country. Bicknells are also found in the Barbadoes and in this country also, some of them rose to the dignity of slaveholders. They generally treated their slaves well, and some of the latter, when they were manumitted, took the name of Bicknell. Hence it appears among the blacks. So no one need go to Africa, said the orator, pleasantly, in search of any ancestors of the Bicknells. Taking up the family in detail, Mr. Bicknell then brought down the descent to the sixth generation from the first Zachary, thus enabling many of those present to trace their lines back to him. He mentioned the Bicknells in New York and in the western part of the State; also those in Maine, where many descendants of Luke are now living. Otis Bicknell was the first of the family in Dalton, and many of the family in Berkshire county are his descendants. Summing up the moral qualities of the family, the speaker regarded them as among the conservative supporters of religion.

After singing by the choir came an address by the Hon. George A. Bicknell, M. C., from Indiana. It was about forty-five minutes long, and the main thought was the value of good blood and the doctrine of inherited traits as illustrated in the Bicknell family. Hence the value of family re-unions from the similarity of family people. The name Bicknell is Scandinavian in origin, and was originally spelt Becknill, or a word which means about the same as Brookville in modern English. The speaker advanced the doctrine that individual greatness arises generally in homogeneous bodies, and the reason that America has produced no great work yet is that the people are not yet sufficiently homogeneous.

This address was followed by a poem by Mrs. A. H. (Bicknell) Ames, of Columbia, Pa., and then came an original hymn written for the occasion and sung to "America," followed by the benediction. After this, dinner was served in the vestry, but the speeches — Mr. Z. L. Bicknell, of East Weymouth, being set down as toast-master — were postponed because of the lateness of the hour. It was voted that the proceedings of the day be published in a pamphlet. Letters were read from Governor Long and the Hon. Marshall P. Wilder. Then Mr. David Bicknell, of London, England, spoke of the English branch of the family, and displayed some portraits. The publication of the family history was ordered, and a committee appointed to oversee the matter. About half-past three the party started in barges to visit the site of old Zachary Bicknell's house, the "King Oak Hill" and the old church and cemetery where the first Bicknells worshipped and were buried. This visit closed the programme of the day.

THE COLLATION.

At the close of the exercises in the audience room of the church, the large company proceeded to the church parlors, where a sumptuous dinner was in readiness, furnished by Mr. H. Blunt, of Boston, the well known and popular caterer. The tables were bountifully spread with hot oysters, meats, cold chickens and turkeys, bread, cake of various sorts, apples, pears, peaches, grapes, etc., ice creams, tea and coffee, and were decorated with elegant bonquets, supplied by the ladies of Weymouth.

Three hundred and forty hungry Bicknells sat down to this welcome repast, made doubly so by keen appetites, whetted by the long hours, and unusual exercise since the morning meal. After grace by the chaplain of the day, a busy scene presented itself, and what with swift flying tongues and active hands the next half hour's work was a scene which the Bicknells of Old or New England never saw before, but which may be only a foretaste of the good things yet to be. The sound of many voices almost drowned the clatter of the dinner service, and—Babel or Pentecost,—there certainly was the gift of strange tongues, suddenly speaking one language in sympathy, in sentiment, and in song. Had not the president possessed full Bicknell stature and a pair of sound, clear lungs, there is doubt whether the dinner hour had not wasted the unspent day; but as the time approached for the departure to the old memorial places of Weymouth, order was restored, although there was the most perfect order before, and the announcement was made that the clock told the hour for retiring, without allowing the privilege of listening to toasts, speeches, songs and poems which had been prepared for the occasion. The president expressed what he knew were the deep regrets of all at the necessity of postponing the after-dinner repast, "the feast of reason and the flow of soul," but comforted all hearts a little by the statement that the unspoken words might yet greet them in print. The following letters were then read from absent invited guests and friends.

LETTERS.

COMMONWEALTH OF MASSACHUSETTS, EXECUTIVE DEPARTMENT,

BOSTON, Aug. 18, 1880.

THOMAS W. BICKNELL. ESQ., 16 Hawley Street, Boston:

DEAR SIR:—I am very much obliged for your kind invitation to attend the re-union of the Bicknell family, to be held at Weymouth on the twenty-second of September next. It comes at the same time with the agricultural fairs, one of which I have already engaged myself to attend, so that I shall be unable to join you. I cannot, however, let the occasion pass without sending my congratulations and best wishes for the occasion. In my native town of Buckfield, Maine, and in the adjoining towns, the name of Bicknell was one of the most frequent and estimable. Those who bore it were men of character and influence. One of them, my old friend Mr. William Bicknell, of Hartford, who I presume will be with you, has distinguished himself there by his pen, and his son, a merchant of Boston, has occupied public positions with credit. There are many others, some of whom still remain in their native State, while the rest, with the push and enterprise characteristic of the family, are now busy in every walk of life in other States.

Please convey to my friends and acquaintances who will be present my kind regards, and my respect for the name they bear, and believe me,

Yours, very truly,

JOHN D. LONG.

HISTORIC GENEALOGICAL SOCIETY.

SOCIETY'S HOUSE. 18 SOMERSET STREET,

BOSTON, MASS., Sept. 9, 1880.

MY DEAR SIR:—Your kind invitation to attend the Bicknell Family Association meeting on the 22d is in hand. Gladly would I accept it, did circumstances permit. There is, in addition to physical inability, the fact that I shall on that day attain to my eighty-second year of life, and cannot leave home.

I beg, however, to assure you that I feel a lively interest in everything that pertains to the treasuring up and perpetuation of the history and genealogy of our New England families. In nothing is the Divine benevolence more fully illustrated than by those ties of fraternal love which bind the family circle together. It is, therefore, a sacred duty to preserve the genealogy of the Bicknell family, and in this effort I bid you God speed. I know of no more pleasant duty to any one who has any regard for his ancestry, than to record the incidents and history of their lives and their relatives. Next to the training of the spirit for the Life Eternal, there can be no more noble service than to treasure up and perpetuate a record of the principles and deeds of our fathers, who have transmitted to us the rich inheritance which we now enjoy.

With great respect,

MARSHALL P. WILDER.

HON. THOS. W. BICKNELL,

President of the Bicknell Family Association.

STATE OF RHODE ISLAND, EXECUTIVE DEPARTMENT,

PAWTUCKET, Aug. 16, 1880.

HON. THOS. W. BICKNELL :

MY DEAR SIR :—I have your kind note of the 12th inst. It would give me pleasure to join you in your re-union at the time and place named. I shall endeavor to do so. If I am not present it will be on account of other engagements already made for that week, or press of business. Can tell later. Thanking you for the invitation.

I am, yours very truly,

A. H. LITTLEFIELD.

MUNROE, ADAMS CO., IND., Sept. 14, 1880.

TO THE SECRETARY OF THE BICKNELL FAMILY GATHERING :

DEAR BROTHER AND RELATIVES :—I received the invitation to attend your gathering too late to get ready in time. But the main trouble is, I am a poor Methodist preacher, and have a wife and five beautiful, sweet and intelligent young Bicknells to support, and it takes about all my salary to support them. I am truly glad to know that I have so many illustrious connection. I should like so much to be with you at your gathering. I am the youngest child of thirteen. My father and mother were born and raised in North Carolina, and remained there after they were married until they had nine children; they then moved to Indiana in the year 1833, where we have since lived. My father died in the city of Indianapolis in 1876. He never had a spell of sickness in his life, except the sickness at his death, which was only twelve hours before he died. My mother is still living; she is seventy-eight years old. Five of our family are dead. I have a brother, Rev. L. W. Bicknell, a Baptist minister. Quite a number of our connection are in Vincennes and Sullivan, Ind., Bicknell's Point, Ill., and in the South. I never heard of a Bicknell being arrested, put in jail or prison in my life. I never knew a Bicknell that was an infidel, and I hope I never may.

Although my grandfather owned a distillery in North Carolina, and my father was raised in a still-house, almost; yet I never heard of, nor saw a Bicknell that was a drunkard. Samuel Bicknell was my grandfather's name. He owned a large plantation in North Carolina and a large number of slaves. Both of my grandfathers were in the Revolutionary war. My father's name was Lewis T. I have an uncle in the South somewhere, by the name of Larkin Bicknell. The Bicknells of our branch are a prolific people. All that I ever knew had large families. Well, I don't know but what the Lord might just as well people this world with Bicknells as anybody else. Oh! I should like to be with you so much. It would do me good every way; but I am one of your poor connections and am not able to come. But I hope that we may all meet in that beautiful city, in that better country, where we shall join in one grand and glorious re-union that shall never end.

Yours fraternally,

I. J. BICKNELL.

STANWIX, ONEIDA COUNTY, N. Y., Sept. 15, 1880.

ALFRED BICKNELL, ESQ., CORRESPONDING SECRETARY, ETC.:

DEAR SIR:— My brother James, the elder, requests me to inform you that your favor of September 10, kindly inviting him to write a letter to be read at the Bicknell family re-union, is received. He says he should be very happy to grant the request, but in consequence of a trembling of the hand, it is quite difficult for him to write, therefore he wishes to be excused; he would be highly gratified to meet with you in your re-union, but age and infirmity are in the way; his good will and prayers are for the success of your gathering.

Very truly yours,

MOSES W. BICKNELL.

Rowe, Mass., Sept. 13, 1880.

To the Honorable Race of Bicknells :

Dear Kinsmen :—I have been invited to be with you in your gathering upon the ancestral grounds of Weymouth. Am sorry not to be able to meet you there, but previous arrangements prevent.

It is gratifying to me that the interest in our numerous family has made this move. If the American Republic understands itself it will henceforth give full recognition to this branch of its constituency. As to our corporate and individual standing, I believe the B's are an industrious and respectable race; outside of jails and poor-houses, at this present writing, I hear of no drones — no one held in durance vile. I think you will find yourselves when assembled upon our very great-grandfather Zach's estate, a very creditable swarm of B's; and so no doubt do our uncles, our aunts, sisters and cousins, all feel the same.

Are we not proud of our ancestry who were, I hear, Norwegian pirates? While everybody in the early times of European sojourn committed depredations upon his neighbor, other people's forefathers skulking behind trees and ignobly never losing sight of land, our progenitors launched boldly and manfully out upon the broad ocean. But why need I say this? Your — our historian, Quincy Bicknell, and our poet, Mrs. Bicknell Ames, will speak and sing what praises are in all modesty our due.

The writer of this would at any time be glad to see any of our tribe at his home in Western Massachusetts — get off at Zoar on the Hoosac Tunnel Railroad, inquire for Rowe. This place is one of the Switzerlands of America, — scenery very fine in summer.

I hope Rev. E. A. Wyman, Ph. D., will be present to speak for our branch of the family.

Very truly and gladly,

W. M. Bicknell.

———

Brick Church, E. Orange, N. J., Sept. 1, 1880.

Mr. T. W. Bicknell :

My Dear Sir :—Yesterday I received your circular giving notice of the proposed Bicknell Re-union, at Weymouth, Mass.

I am not certain that I can lay claim to a place in your Association, as I am not a direct descendant of Zachary, but most certainly I am from one branch of the Bicknell family, and am quite convinced that we are from the same respectable old stock.

I well remember, when a boy, hearing my grandfather (Wm. Bicknell) tell of a visit he had made to Taunton, Somersetshire, for the purpose of tracing

5

the pedigree of the family. After his death in 1825, I saw and read the account in his own handwriting. * * * * *

He found by searching the Parish Church records, that a branch of the family (probably Zachary Bicknell) had emigrated to America soon after its first settlement. * * * * * * *

My great-grandfather, John Bicknell, was a native of Taunton, but settled in London early in life. * * * * *

You are at liberty to make what use you please of the account herewith.

You will please present my affectionate regards to every member of our numerous family, and believe me.

Yours very truly,

DAVID BICKNELL.

BRICK CHURCH, E. ORANGE, N. J., Sept. 7, 1880.

MR. T. W. BICKNELL :

MY DEAR SIR :—Many thanks for your prompt and very kind acknowledgment of my letter, addressed to the Secretary of your Association, A. Bicknell, Esq.

As I expect to start in a new business this month in New York, I may not be able to attend the Re-union and in the event of my not being there I will forward to your address, by the 15th inst., the picture of my dear, old grandfather (Wm. Bicknell) and his two sons, my father (W. J.) and my uncle (Elhanan). The latter was an opulent oil merchant of London. I copy the following from " Cooper's Biographical Dictionary ":

BICKNELL, ELHANAN,

A great patron of Art, died at his residence on Herne Hill, Camberwell, Nov. 27, 1861. He was engaged in commercial pursuit, and the personal property left at his decease was sworn at Doctors Commons as under £350,000. The wealth which he acquired was liberally, judiciously, and unostentatiously spent, not upon himself alone (for even the beautiful specimens of Art which enriched his mansion were freely open to others besides his personal friends), but in doing good to those who stood in need of help.

There is another fact connected with my family which I omitted in my last letter. My grandfather, after being at Mr. Wesley's School at Kingswood, was removed to St. Savior's grammar school, founded by Queen Elizabeth. At that school he met a boy bearing his name, William Bicknell, and they became great friends, but could never trace any relationship. When my grandfather sold out his business in Blackman street, Southwark, it was to his old schoolmate, William Bicknell, second.

I think the Bicknells can show a good record for respectability.

I am, Yours very truly,

DAVID BICKNELL.

HARTFORD, ME., Sept. 16, 1880.

COUSIN ALFRED BICKNELL :—The following is at your disposal.

If the oldest living great-grandson (by the name of Bicknell) of Nathaniel Bicknell and the oldest grandson of Col. Luke Bicknell (by the name of Bicknell) and the oldest son of William Bicknell entitle me Patriarch of this branch of the Bicknell family, then I accept the title, and when an invitation from you, to be present at a Bicknell meeting at Weymouth in September, my heart was filled with joy, for I had long seen, by a prophetic eye, that the Bicknell blood, coursing in the veins of live Bicknells, would have such a meeting. But the mature judgment of seventy-seven years, and the *counsel* of her, whom I have lived with in married life fifty-two years this month, said, "You must let well enough alone," eclipses all my long cherished anticipations of being present in body. If the mind be strong, it cannot carry the lame tenement to the long wished for Association. Shall I give a brief statement of my three named ancestors, including their wives?

Nathaniel died at Abington, Mass., at the age of seventy-nine, in 1804, the year I made my first appearance at Hanover street, Boston, in a select party consisting of my mother and her assistants — mother at the age of twenty years. Luke died on the farm on which he was born in 1814, at the age of sixty-five, while holding the office of clerk of Abington. I, a child of ten years, knew him but to love grandfather, one whom the town and church delighted to honor. William died at Turner, Me., 1841, aged sixty years, after filling offices of trust in Turner and Hartford. I stood, as a father, beside his death-bed, and heard him say, "William, I shall pass to that immortal shore where all is blessed, where all will sing redeemed by Love."

I knew my great-grandmother, Elizabeth Lincoln Bicknell; she died at Abington, 1822, aged ninety-four years. I was long acquainted with my grandmother, Olive Gurney Bicknell, "truly a mother in Israel." She died at Hartford, Me., a pensioner in 1845, at the age of ninety-five years. She and her husband, worthy members of Center Church, Abington, near where they reared a family of eight to manhood. My mother, Martha Bosson, married my father in 1803, at Boston, died at her youngest daughter's, Mrs. Joseph F. Paul, Boston, February, 1879, at the age of ninety-five, expressing a desire to depart from earth-life to that immortal state where the good-bye is never known. I bid mother good-bye in 1878, believing we should never meet again in earth-life. I received a farewell blessing at the age of nearly seventy-six from a mother who was twenty years my senior in age. From my residence in Hartford, Me., her remains, accompanied by my sister Mrs. Paul, her son George, at the age of twenty, an infant when his grandmother made his home her home, were interred at Turner, Me., beside my father, her first husband, after an address by Rev. Mr. French, of that town. I saw, on that day I left mother at J. F. Paul's, at the same time, on a flight of stairs leading to the dining-room, four generations, mother, oldest son, grandson and great-grandchild.— a rare sight for a son to see at seventy-five years. I was well acquainted with my father's brothers and sisters, their

wives and husbands and children. Captain Nathaniel, grandfather of Rev.
G. W. Bicknell, died 1872. aged ninety-five years; married Elizabeth Rams-
dell; of eight children, only one living. Noah died 1872, aged eighty-nine
years; married Nancy Brown; of eight children. James, Alfred and Deborah,
Mrs. H. W. Noyes, are living. Luke died 1870, aged eighty-three years;
married Deborah Corbett; of five children I knew, Luke and Angeline
are living. James died 1862, aged seventy-two years; married Rebecca
Bates, Vesta Howard, Sophia Willey; of two sons by the first wife. Henry is
living. Elizabeth died 1853, aged seventy-seven years; married Robert Bates
of Weymouth; children are living — Capt. James H., aged eighty years, one
of the best boot makers ever in Weymouth on face stitch work; Robert, aged
seventy-eight years. Rebecca died 1847, aged fifty-five years; married Josiah
Cushman; of four children William is living. Robert Bates, Henry Bicknell
and William Cushman voted in the same ballot box on the 13th that my son
Henry A. and I did.

I would not forget my family of five children, four are living. William E.,
our first born, must speak for himself. Julia C. married Melvander G.
Forbes, died at Buckfield, Me., 1870, married 1854, leaving two daughters
who were sophomores at Bates College, both teaching the second terms in
Hartford this season, youngest will soon return to college. Henry Augustus
married Miss Abbie M. Mason, of Buckfield, Me., whom we live with on the
old homestead. Hattie Augusta, twin mate of Henry A., married William
L. Morrill of Buckfield. Both were married 1874 by Rev. Mr. Munson.
Rachel died 1853, aged seventy-three years; married Capt. John Noyes; of
children, John, Luke, Nathaniel and Holland W. are living.

I received a card on the evening of the 15th from Hon. T. W. Bicknell, saying he would be pleased to receive a letter from me in prose or verse. I send
an article, "What is Life?" If it is worthy of the occasion and not egotism
in me I should like to have it read by my grandson, Edward Bicknell.

My limited time to comply with your request must be an excuse for errors.

WILLIAM BICKNELL.

What is Life?

A breath, a moment, a day or an hour?
Or is it some dream of years gone by?
For one, I have seen a reality,
That no dream can paint, with the bright colors
Of experience.
My footsteps, from a mere childhood to manhood,

Have trod in many paths, which only
Can be hid, when reason is dethroned.
I have acted a part in three scenes in
The great drama of life. A loved child,
Parent, and grandparent. Have trod the paths
Of youth in its variety. Have drank from
That fount of Education, to which all
Look back from manhood, even from old age,
With that mournful pleasure, that no one
But a participator in that boon
Can ever know.

          For who can speak the joys
Of New England's school-days, but her scholars?
The happiness, that has been confined
Within the walls of some old school-room,
Where both sexes, from the child of four years
To him who stood forth in all his manhood,
Were subject to him, whose eye was their law,
Never can be painted by mortals.
          Oh happy days!
Do you not love to dwell upon the past,
And review those scenes, in which Nature
Was drawn in all its brilliant colors?
Methinks I can now almost hear the rap, rap,
For silence, from our honored master, which
Has been broken by some well known truant,
Who had longed for, and now must receive
The ferule of those good old days.
I have acted a part in the next scene.
A fond parent has been doubly blest*
With that charge, which has been so little studied,
The responsibility of training
Children in the way of life.

          I once smiled upon a loved son,†
And saw death touch his beauteous form,
Which was a passport for his pure spirit

---

* Twins now thirty-seven years old.
† Edward Everett died aged 17 months

To his God—to my God—through His dear Son
The third and last scene!

The untried paths of parents are being trod
By children of my youth. They love to point,
With a parent's love, to these buds of manhood,
Which are blessings lent.

Life is not a dream
To one who has seen so many blessings.

I have seen the hand of God
In those flowers and thorns which beset my path.
God has been my shield and buckler.
By Faith, I see the Light which points me
To the immortal scene of glory, where
Each actor will join the great chorus
Redeemed by Grace—in honor of the Lamb.

WM. BICKNELL.

HARTFORD, ME., Sept. 16, 1880.

CEDAR SPRINGS, MICH., Sept. 15, 1880.

To the BICKNELL FAMILY ASSOCIATION: GREETING:

Members of our family wishing to be represented at the great family
gathering, request me to send this brief communication.

Otis, the sixth from Zachary, with Molly Stoddard his wife, removed from
Abington about the year 1791, to Dalton, Berkshire County, Mass. They
raised nine children. The five boys early imbibed radical temperance and
anti-slavery principles. The oldest, James Bicknell, my father, believes he
raised the first barn in Berkshire County, that was raised without rum. He
is still living, active and sprightly, though past his fourscore; still interested
in politics and in religion, for he has always linked the two together. His
life has been a very useful one. He wishes to be remembered at your great
feast and we all regret our inability to be present.

With great respect for the family name and all who honor it, I remain,

Yours fraternally,

C. C. BICKNELL,
Missionary Am. S. S. Union.

TOASTS AND RESPONSES.

Z. L. BICKNELL, ESQ., TOAST-MASTER.

OLD WEYMOUTH.

The mother of many noted sons. The Bicknells claim a large place at the household hearth, and a warm place near the motherly heart; we rejoice in her prosperity, and see in it the good, healthy growth of Bicknell blood in her ancestral stock.

RESPONSE BY T. H. HUMPHREY, ESQ.

Mr. President, Ladies and Gentlemen:

This ancient town has indeed been the mother of many noble sons and daughters, of whom she may well be proud. Her history of more than two hundred and fifty years, has been neither an uneventful nor an unimportant one. Her own modest records give the names of many of those children to whom she owes her present prosperous condition, yet they chronicle but few of their deeds, while other tongues and other pens have neither been silent nor idle in proclaiming their praises.

Many are the names among her children of once numerous and honored families, that are now known only in the musty leaves of parchment, or upon the less enduring gravestone. Many more are the names of those who were born upon her soil and nurtured by her fostering hand, and who have carried to other places the remembrances of their birthplace, where they have contributed by industry, skill and upright bearing, to the success and renown of the towns of their adoption. They carried away, with her lessons of integrity and thrift, the mother's blessing, and they send back, from time to time, the kindly greeting of well loved children to an honored parent. In their character and life they uphold the reputation of the mother who bore them, and bear faithful witness of her fidelity and love. But none the less dear and esteemed are the names of those sons and daughters who have remained by the old homestead, and who have stood by the mother through good and through evil report, who have shared her peril and her prosperity; and who have, in ten generations, lifted their venerated town from a few scattered dwellings on the borders of the sea, to its present proud and prosperous position,—the product of their toil and privations, and the fulfilment of their hopes.

It is not for the parent to single out as the object of special eulogy, any one of her numerous offspring, all equally her own, and all perhaps equally deserving of her regard; but she can hardly refrain from uttering words of affection and commendation as the birthday of any one of them approaches, and the brothers and sisters all heartily unite in these evidences of good feeling, when, otherwise, there might spring up jealousies and discontent.

And, so, to-day, does "Old Weymouth" welcome with peculiar assurances of regard, this festival day of one of her always present families, who came among the earliest, and who, from that day to this, have never failed to strive with generous emulation in extending the usefulness and renown of their ever honored and cherished mother. The name of Bicknell, from the day of Zachary the elder, whose early death cast a gloom over the infant settlement, from the day of John the patriarch, his son, down through the generations to the present time, has been one of credit and power, to which its compatriots could point with pride and satisfaction. Not only has it done its part in sustaining the dignity and reputation of its birthplace, in the persons of those who remained at home, but it has sent out its shoots into the far corners of the land, and there transplanted branches have as well, sustained the record they carried with them; and Weymouth, to-day, gladly recognizes the value of their services.

And it is with no ordinary feelings of satisfaction and enjoyment, that the mother expresses her hearty sympathy in the object of this gathering to-day, as she offers her sincere congratulations to the members of the family who live within her borders, with her cordial welcome to those who come to this festival from other homes, to enjoy the hospitality of the paternal hearthstone.

May the mother and the children never lose this assurance of mutual confidence and esteem, but may the bond of union grow stronger and stronger with the passage of the years.

OUR INVITED GUESTS.

The Bicknell latch string is always out, and a warm welcome invites you to the hospitable circle. The Bicknell girls have often entertained angels—not unawares—and we offer to our invited guests, not only a choice seat at the table, but many chances to enter the fold and become one of us.

RESPONSE BY REV. D. P. LEAVITT,

M. E. Church, East Weymouth.

The invited guests share the pleasure of these festivities, notwithstanding the misfortune of not being born Bicknells. The assurance of a chance to enter the fold comes too late to many a guest, since other folds have been invaded, and such chances as these were have been already taken.

A great statesman of this country once said that "there is a moral and philosophical respect for our ancestors which elevates the character and improves the heart." The Bicknell family to-day recognize this truth, and their outside friends gladly unite with them in paying honor to the worthy men whose sturdy virtues were the foundation of that character in their descendants which has given honor to the Bicknell name in the past, and which promises to perpetuate it with increasing lustre in the future.

OUR ENGLISH COUSINS.

We came out from them, and are still of them. The new American stock takes pride in its old English home and kin, and hopes never to dishonor the family name and birthright. We welcome to our board a lineal descendant of our English fathers. Jehovah Jirah has been our motto and Mizpeh our prayer.

RESPONSE BY MR. DAVID BICKNELL, NEW JERSEY.

MR. PRESIDENT AND FRIENDS:

It is very gratifying to me after sojourning in this country for over thirty years, to come so suddenly amongst so many of my own name and kin.

I now realize the promise of a Bicknell welcome if I attended this first social gathering of the Bicknell family.

I thank you, sir, most sincerely for so kindly proposing my health and the friends for so warmly responding.

Independent of being introduced as an English Bicknell, my tongue must now have told the same tale, not only that I am an Englishman, but also a *Cockney.*

Each county in England has its own peculiar dialect. London has hers. The Rev. R. Hill objected to dropping the "h" as it would make him 'ill (or sick) all his life. I never had that fear and have never been under medical treatment since I was an infant, then the doctor did his best to kill me, but finally gave up, left the house, but not hearing of my death he returned after waiting two or three days, and seeing I still lived, called me a "little humbug." I have managed to dodge the doctor ever since, and propose to do the same for some years to come, that I may enjoy the pleasure of meeting with you in this social family way.

The account you have listened to respecting my branch of the Bicknell family is very imperfect — but I hope, within a short time, to furnish the link that will again unite us.

There is one thing about this gathering of the Bicknell family that is particularly pleasing to my mind. Although a Congregationalist in principle, a Presbyterian in practice, I am glad that you are meeting in this M. E. Church, as it brings to mind so many of my family who were intimately connected with Methodism from its very foundation. And where is a fitter place than the house of God to remember all the way which the Lord our God has led us these many forty years in the wilderness.

May we continue to acknowledge the God of our fathers. It will then always be morning with us. The night will never come.

OUR PATRIARCHS.

Old age wears a crown of glory, when found in the ways of righteousness. We bow down before the gray-haired veterans, and honor our ancestry which has borne so many octogenarians, men and women who have lived long and well, know how to die well.

RESPONSE BY REV. F. P. CHAPIN,

Pastor Congregational Church, North Weymouth.

MR. PRESIDENT AND MEMBERS OF THE FAMILY:

There is a saying that it becomes a Scotchman to look well how he makes up his mind, for when he once puts his foot down, it is hard for him to take it up again. This saying has reference to the well known trait of the

Scotch generally for consistency and persistency. I thought after listening awhile to the admirable portraits of character drawn of several of your ancestors, before I knew where the Bicknell family originated, that surely you must be of Scotch descent. I was taken aback when I learned that you were originally Scandinavian. But respect for my opinion returned when one of your speakers said that the family, after leaving Scandinavia, actually spent some time in Scotland, before going to England, so your ancestors gained the best traits of those nations before coming to America.

I think your ancestor John must have put his foot down right when he became prominent in church and parish matters in 1651. I am glad to find by the Parish Records that so many of his descendants followed in his footsteps. This appears quite evident from the fact that none of them have been committed for crime.

I am glad to meet so many descendants of one of the early members of the First Church of Weymouth. The old church salutes you, and feels a material joy and pride in your gathering. In response to the sentiment which you gave me to reply to, and which your ancestors have so remarkably illustrated, let me say in the words of wisdom : "*Length of days is in her right hand ; and in her left hand riches and honor. Her ways are ways of pleasantness, and all her paths are peace. She is a tree of life to them that lay hold upon her ; and happy is every one that retaineth her.*"

I thank you for the very kind invitation which I received and for what I have enjoyed at your gathering, and for this opportunity to add my mite to the record of this day.

THE BICKNELL DESCENT.

" Blood is thicker than water."

RESPONSE BY ELLERY BICKNELL CRANE, WORCESTER, MASS.

MR. PRESIDENT, FELLOW KINSMEN AND FRIENDS :

I am really disappointed at being selected to respond to the sentiment just announced and feel that your President has made a great mistake in his selection this time, for the reason of my inability to do justice to the subject in hand. It calls for something to be said in behalf of the female portion of the Bicknell family, and they certainly deserve a more worthy and complimentary response than I can utter in their behalf.

This is a gathering of Bicknells of which we can justly be proud. But we must remember that they all do not bear that name here to-day and were those of your committee to deny those of us who do not answer to that name the privilege of being represented at this family gathering it would be doing a great injustice to a very large if not the largest share of the Bicknell family. But your committee has shown wisdom by making the invitation broad, *blood* being the shibboleth by which we are admitted and we join with you heartily in ascribing honor to our noble and respected Bicknell ancestry.

I have no doubt that there are some here to day who would term it a serious loss to be without the Bicknell name, for they are deservedly proud of it, but the record shows that since the death of Zachary there have been found those of the family who were willing to sacrifice the name, but not the blood for the good of mankind, and I know those generous souls may be found to-day. It has been proposed that there should be written and published a genealogical history of the Bicknell family. This gathering bespeaks encouragement and success to such an undertaking and we must give our individual support to the work, and aid our good and worthy cousin, Quincy Bicknell, Esq., all we can, who I know is the right man in the right place, and will give us a record such as every member of the family will take pride in possessing. There is great difficulty in tracing family blood without the name, so that those of us who belong to the female lines should see to it, that these branches are still vigorous and thrifty portions of the great family tree. We know they make noble women, excellent wives and the very best of mothers, always found ready to perform well their part in the onward march of progress, and although little may appear on the printed page concerning our noble mothers, volumes in commendation have been written, and will be written upon the hearts of their children.

OUR CLERGY.

The flock is scattered, but the fold is one. The Bicknell shepherds have a busy work to gather them in, but their reward is sure.

RESPONSE BY REV. GEO. W. BICKNELL, LOWELL, MASS.

Mr. President and Members of the Bicknell Family Association:

I should act false to my own feelings did I not emphasize in the very outset of my remarks, the sentiment which, above all others, sways me at this time, and which has been uttered so often to-day. I am glad, very glad, to be here upon this occasion. In common, no doubt, with you all, I have looked forward to this gathering with very many pleasant anticipations. The reality has eclipsed even the brightest. Every thing has conspired to make this day, as our honored President has expressed it, " A red-letter day of our calendar." Nature smiles as we love to see her, when we want a real good time. It is neither too warm nor too cool — just right. The Bicknell heads are clear as has been made evident in the eloquent addresses of the day, and the perfect arrangements of the committee who have had this gathering in charge, who have surprised and more than pleased us, ministering unto our tastes, expectations and appetites in a manner which must be acceptable to every one. I am satisfied — doubly so — with every thing I have seen, heard and tasted, except the part which I am now expected to take in this glorious reunion. It is no effort — nay, but a pleasure, to which I cannot give expression, to take you, whom I have known, and also you whom I have never seen before, by the hand, ask all manner of questions about your families, and never be thought impertinent, and tell you all I know about others — good things I mean; and I do not believe there are many evil things associated with the Bicknell name; but this making a speech after one of the best efforts of a day (eating such a hearty dinner) is almost too much. But I will try and be short, — I mean in my speech.

I am asked to respond to the toast, " Our Clergy." I only wish I knew more about them. The only one with whom I have any acquaintance, and possibly not so much as I ought to have even with him, when we endeavor to fulfil literally the command of a writer, " Know thyself "— is your humble speaker. I do not think it best to say much about him. With all my failings, I am modest. To-day I do not want to occupy any position, where I shall be regarded as out of place, as " one of the boys at home." And as I stand on this spot to-day, and through the eye of retrospection, see the long line of Bicknells reaching from the right resting on 1635, to the left resting on 1880, and remember that my great big double big grandfather here lived and died, and did what many of his grandsons probably hate to do, cut, or sawed his own wood, and tilled the soil round about us, I do almost feel at home, though never before have I set foot on this ground—hallowed by so many associations, and, to many of you, pleasant remembrances. But the Bicknell line has had in the past (and there are several of the same class in the present), a number who have spent their lives in preaching, and it is to be hoped, also in practising. I do not know, for I have no authority for the statement, but I will venture to guess, that each generation has had its appointed share of men, who can be properly classed under the subject our honored toast-master has given me. I have often thought —(and now with Bicknell caution, I propose to make a perfectly safe statement)— that the life of the older clergyman years ago— before the remembrance, it may be, of any of these young men under seventy before me, must have been a very pleasant, or a very unpleasant one. There cannot have been any half way about the matter. There was an awe surrounding the profession, a made up and put on sanctity — the work of many years — which must have been pleasing, or displeasing to the occupant. It would have been terrible galling to me any way. The minister was way up in the pulpit — higher up than the modern pulpit puts a man, unless he is very, very tall. He never laughed (he must have been an odd one of our race however), but he was austere, stern, and in some senses, unapproachable. In a great degree he was the oracle of the community in which he resided — his *say* frequently law. Pastoral calls, if I am to believe all that I have been told, struck terror to the young, and filled the mature with agitation. I should like to have seen a Bicknell in the old time regimen. I wonder if children did actually run to wood-houses and barns, or seek refuge in the folds of mothers' dresses when they saw him coming. I am confident that it didn't require matrons so long to get ready .to receive the minister as in the present day of ———, you know the routine of preparation. Yet there was, generally speaking, a roundness of life, a purity of character. a solidity in the clergy of olden time, which made even their human personalities, models of excellence; and which it will be well for us all never to forget, but after which we might, in some measure, well pattern.

We have at the present time. several clergymen bearing our name, who are reported to be earnest workers in the Kingdom of Christ. But it is a matter of pleasure to note, that the clergyman of to-day is of, and in the masses. By this I mean, that he lives and moves more among and with the people. He makes religion, by his walk, teaching, and example, less of a bugbear than as once it was regarded. Not that he has lost the true dignity of manhood, but he has lost (and I am glad of it) some of the powers of freezing, of repelling, of ecclesiastical importance, which formerly characterized the ministry. If he is a true man, he goes out with a heart to meet hearts — a soul to meet souls — to minister unto the spiritual wants of the day, more than to impress people with his individual importance and sanctity, even if he possessed them. People are not so much afraid of the clergyman as in the days gone by: and upon the other hand. one of the main things to be desired now is, that he shall be so strong in his convictions of truth and right — that in no sense shall *he* be afraid of the people. The man who is afraid to speak his honest convictions upon questions of vital importance where he honestly believes them truth, to secure advancement, is a poor sort of a man and a mean minister. While I believe that the people have as much respect for the ministerial office as ever, yet it is pleasant to see awe melting away, and warmness glowing from it. There is to-day, so far as my observation extends — more mutual sympathy between pastors and people — more readiness to bear one another's burdens — more mingling of brotherly love and interest — a more delightful association — a warmer heart beating than must have characterized the association of years ago. And the influence must be equally as good. if not better. I may stand in awe of a man (I say I *may* but I don't); but awe never inspired that feeling for which humanity yearns to-day—love. To love him, I want to feel that he has an interest in, or a brotherly feeling toward me. I do not care how kindly a man may *feel*, if he is exteriorly cold, repellant toward me, he can, like the old priest of Scripture record, run over to the other side just as quick as he wants to. He can hurt my feelings *most* by coming close to me. The clergy are fast recognizing the truth, that it is vastly better to have the affections of the people, than their mere respect, or obsequiousness. While as a consequence, I say again. the ministerial office is not surrounded in the frigidity of the past, it is enveloped with a desire for human good, which the people see and understand, and thanking heaven for lives consecrated to the uplifting of humanity, their own affections are quickened and inspired. and they bring to the labor their own hearts, and crown the work, to which the minister only lends his aid, with the glorious fruitage of their own purified lives and souls.

It may be said, properly perhaps, that the Bicknell clergy have not been dilatory in recognizing the advancements of the day. So far as I know, the better interpretations of life and duty, as well as of belief, have not been cast aside. The period of scholarship has found devoted students. While, it may be, upon some of the really non-essentials of theology, they may not be all of one mind, yet upon essentials, upon everything which advances the human family, there is probably agreement. We disagree upon matters of which men know the least. If we would all work in directions with which we are acquainted, where, too, men are generally agreed, and which afford labors enough to keep us all busy during this life, and in the discharge of which, we are receiving much of our preparation for the next sphere of being, I think the world would be happier and better than it is. But be that as it may, the clergy, and so far as I know, the family of our name have not turned their backs upon human good. I do not think any Bicknell would sanction the hanging of a criminal, especially if the public good could be protected otherwise, no matter how much he might reverence the laws or customs of antiquity. I do not think any Bicknell would sanction the burning of heretics, or condemnation to prison of any differing in religious faith from himself. We have connections in the Baptist, Methodist, Unitarian, Episcopalian, Universalist, and I do not know how many other denominations—yet all indicating theological advancement over the interpretations of a century or two ago. They are all at work for the upbuilding of Christianity; and this I desire to say here, as I have often said in public before, no matter whether they believe upon some matters as I do or not, working as you are, brother clergymen, for human advancement, for intellectual development among men, to foster spiritual culture, religious growth and to secure a blessed salvation for human souls, I say with my whole heart, God bless you; and though we may be in different corps of the grand army, yet the success of your banner, indicating victory over sin and wrong, shall fill me with as great joy as may the triumph of my own. It is not for sectarian success for which we are to fight and labor. Shame on the man whose object is that alone; but the true aim should be to do what we can to aid in securing the triumph of truth over ignorance and error, love over hate, and Christ over every antagonism.

So far as I know, all which has in view the liberation of men from slavery —the freedom of the mind from bondage—the reign of purity in social life, in the ballot, in government, aye everywhere, has found in our clergy, earnest and warm support.

I have never yet met one who might be termed a bigoted Bicknell. I take it for granted that there are none among the clergy of the family. I hope not. I do not know, however, that there is a Bicknell who has not firm convictions upon important, or to him, interested subjects. Yet firmness may not be bigotry. A man can fully believe that he is in the right in his political or religious views, and yet not be intolerant. For myself I hope never to assume that Pharisaical view of superiority in opinion, which will not enable me to treat with respect, and honor the men who may differ from me; and may never any Bicknell take such a stand. Whatever our special office, service, or thought may be, co-operation in the great work of human advancement is ever essential. One cannot say that there is no need of the other. Yet this I believe, if there was a better understanding pertaining to matters of individual or sectarian belief, there would be infinitely less antagonism among religious bodies than there is in the present.

The clergyman is, by his profession, a preacher; and yet, dear members of the Bicknell Family Association, you are all in reality, preachers. By man's hands you may not have received the rite of ecclesiastical ordination; but by God, each and every human soul is an ordained preacher. The long lines reaching so far down the past, have all been preachers. Their lives have taught the glories and beauties of honor and virtue; and the strength and respectability of our honored family, owe much to their grand life sermons. They may not have swayed multitudes, and you may not move masses; but some have heard, and have been profited. Yes, by life which should be pure and sacred—by example which should be bright and glowing, reflecting in a degree, yet as well as mortal may, the radiance of Him who made human existence glorious and resplendent with almost the beauty of the heavenly—by word which should be inspired by the spirit of purity—by act which should draw in its life force from Christ himself—by influence which, while exercising its action on earth, shall gain its strength from on high—by attainments which may be as stepping stones to the eternal and the real—by struggles which have for their goal, the reaching of grander conditions for living than these occupied by man—by victories which shall enable the soul to realize its nobler possibilities—by characters rounded, full, complete, blessing earth, and which may shine in the remembrance of humanity long after the framework in which they are now moulding, shall have passed from human vision—yes, by all which goes to make up a nobler manhood and a brighter, purer womanhood, we are all preachers, members of Christ's clergy; and if we are faithful as we ought to be, when our earth work is completed, and the bright angel of God's love shall conduct us through the shaded valley to the bright summerland beyond, to the home where we may learn more of God, of love, of truth, and be blessed with associations for which our souls hope and yearn, the silvery voice will whisper words rich with approval, which may bestow upon us joys worthy of the immortal realm, and which will a thousand fold reward us for every toil, sacrifice, and effort of the present.

OUR BUSINESS MEN.

Industrious, honest, energetic, successful. They are all busy "B's" without a drone in the hive, and lay up more honey than money.

RESPONSE BY MR. ALFRED BICKNELL, BOSTON.

MR. PRESIDENT AND COUSINS ALL:

It certainly gives me very great pleasure to meet so many of our family here to-day. We had hoped for a pleasant day and for a goodly number, but this day and this large audience exceeds our most sanguine expectations. I accept it as an augury of a pleasant and useful and far-reaching work for our Association in the future. I have always felt a pride in our *name*, and in our family reputation so far as I knew it; but not until since I have been engaged with our President and others in this work, have I understood so fully the solid basis for a just pride. As letters from different sections of the country came to us, all telling the same story,—no black sheep, no bummers in our camp, all self-supporting, reliable, square-dealing people,—I confess I *was* decidedly elated, and with reason too. You know that the saying " An honest man is the noblest work of God " is generally accepted as truth. But I am inclined to think it will bear some modification. I question whether an " honest *family* is not *nobler?*" And I think we can properly claim that ours *is* an honest family. What better title to nobility do we need? What characteristic does " gentle " blood properly impart if not to cause its possessors to follow the teachings of the "golden rule "? And in a remarkable degree I am sure that our great family in all the years that have elapsed since the " ASSURANCE " cast anchor in Boston Harbor and in all the localities up and down this broad land in which we have lived and labored, I am sure that our family *have* followed this precept in their every-day practice very faithfully.

You have asked me, Mr. President, to speak to the sentiment " our business men." Now, you all know that there are at least *two* maxims, or rules, by which business men are governed in their daily dealings. For those who are governed by one only can I respond. We have a class of business men, much more numerous than I could wish, very smart, intelligent in every thing appertaining to money making, keen and sharp in trade, who will tell you that to " buy as *low* as you can, and sell as *high* as you can " is a business duty. They hold that " all is fair in trade," and are always ready with some excuse, plausible to themselves, for any scheme of sharp practice or over-reaching by which they can " make a dollar." They are shrewd, sagacious, unscrupulous, careful to technically observe the requirements of statute law, holding that such compliance completes the sum of their obligations to their fellow men. Such people represent one class. I cannot answer for them. You know them, and no doubt somewhat of their operations. They may be *rich*, many of them are, but their riches are of the kind that sometimes take to themselves wings. Their level of business principles, I do not believe in. And my pride in our family is predicated largely upon the fact, as it seems to me, that *our* folks have *not* been governed by such influences. We have on the contrary recognized the rightfulness, the justice, the duty of giving an equivalent for all our acquisitions. It is said that " exchange is no robbery," and among people honestly organized it is true. But it is sometimes possible for worldly shrewd people by the exercise of a little business diplomacy to exchange a dime for a quarter! It is greatly to the credit of *our* family that we have not engaged in nor encouraged that practice. You have heard the story to-day coming from all quarters, no criminals, no paupers, no imbeciles in *our* family. We may add, with our hearts swelling with honest pride, no swindlers, no sharpers, no Shylocks, either. As I thank my God for his great favor as evidenced in this fruitful land, this advanced civilization and

6

all these instrumentalities for individual and associated improvement and
elevation, so I thank Him fervently for the greater favor shown our family
in their organization and development in the matter of personal integrity.
Many a marble column bears the record of the virtues of the great and good,
but as for me no prouder inscription could I ask than the simple words,
"He was an honest man." Far be it from me to deprecate the accumulation
of wealth by proper means. Be sober — prudent — cautious— industrious—
frugal—pains-taking— but *not sharp*.

I know that every one of our name and descent is familiar with the
prayer of Agur,—"give me neither poverty nor riches." Whether they
realized it or no, I see clearly that the spirit of that prayer, like the key-
note in music, has run through our family since those far away days, hundreds and hundreds of years ago, when our very *name* itself was evolved
from humble beginnings—and if our good Historian with the effective assist-
ance of our President and of our English Cousin, whom we are all delighted to
meet here to-day, shall have the skill and patience to trace our genealogy
back far enough, I am confident that they will find that Agur himself was a
Bicknell, or had Bicknell blood in his veins! But I trespass upon this precious time, and I will close by giving you my version of the underlying principles that I feel have controlled our family practices hitherto, and which I
hope will govern, not *us* alone, but eventually, the whole human family:

> Every day, in every trade,
> Act the vows on Sunday made,
> Make your every word and deed
> Prove the soundness of your creed.
> If word or purse must suffer loss,
> Keep your word good at any cost;
> Your gold may vanish in a day,
> True words and deeds will live alway.

RESPONSE BY MR. A. J. BICKNELL, NEW YORK.

MR. PRESIDENT AND MEMBERS OF OUR FAMILY:

The business men of our branch of the Bicknell family have, so far as I
know, been only moderately successful, but I am pleased to add that as business men their record is good.

OUR LEGISLATORS.

The Bicknells are born rulers. At home they rule with love, tempered with
a strong will; in society they rule with intelligence; in the church with godly
fear, and in the State they rule with integrity, honor and true statesmanship.

RESPONSE BY HON. GEO. A. BICKNELL, INDIANA.

Our Legislators are such as the people require them to be.

If the people demand intelligence and learning and honor, these can readily be found; if the people are satisfied with ignorance and false pretences and venal trickery, these, also, can readily be found.

In general, the representative is better than the worst of his constituents and scarcely equal to the best of them.

If there is any deficiency in him it is the fault of his constituents who ought to have made a better choice. If there is any excellency in him, his constituents have the honor of their wise selection.

Let us hope that in the general progress of our institutions, "our Legislators" and their constituents will alike occupy higher ground in the future than they have reached in the past.

OUR TEACHERS.

The school-house has been the support and the supporter of the Bicknell race. Illiteracy is unknown among our name, and the schools of America have reason to rejoice in the Bicknell educators, who have not only learned, but taught the three R's, and have in various spheres illustrated the grand truths of intelligent thinking, temperate living and consecrated service.

RESPONSE BY MR. THOMAS W. BICKNELL.

Mr. Toast-Master:

That the Bicknell blood has good qualities, we have abundant evidence in the intelligent company before us, which is only a tithe of the same sort of the great army of our name and blood, who are at their homes. That it has the elements of that superior grade, which inspires poets and teachers, there is also the clearest proof from family history and from our experiences of this memorable hour; and if the samples of genius to-day displayed by the Bicknells but reveal the latent talent of the family, we may never know how many "mute, inglorious Miltons," or Aschams may have "lived unwept and died unsung." Our learned historian has modestly stated that the literary element in our Bicknell stock *was monopolized* by Zachary and Thomas of the third generation, while John was left *without this most valuable birthright.* That our honors are tolerably easy and that the talent and scholarship were quite evenly distributed, however, is manifest in the fact, that John's sons and daughters claim the historian, the chaplain and the poets of the day, while the children of Zachary and Thomas share the other honors. Now as near as I can learn the facts, the school-masters' honors are also as equally distributed along the several lines of our descent, and all of our teachers that are not with us at the home circle to-day are "abroad" on missions of valuable service to men. It is quite remarkable what a host of instructors of youth has sprung from the loins of Zachary and Agnes. I believe there are teachers of our blood in half the States of the Union, and they are unusually good and successful ones too; and there are reasons for it. For first, the Bicknells are an intelligent race. While we have never known a *criminal* of our name, we have never known *an illiterate Bicknell*. The Bicknell who was ever obliged to make his *mark* for his autograph has been among the unknown, while hundreds have made their *marks* on unruly and troublesome boys. A natural love of, and desire for, knowledge is a characteristic of our people, and added to that element of intellectual acquisitiveness, has been that other sure qualification of a good teacher, a benevolence that leads to the quickening of other minds to possess the same truth. To acquire but not to hold, has been a principle of the Bicknells, universally,— no misers in wealth or knowledge. Freely receiving and freely giving have been the practice of the family.

Another element possessed in large measure by our race is the natural power to govern. *Home rule* has been an ancestral principle. Well-ordered homes show that we are born-rulers. The ideal of our family discipline has been to foster early self-control; hence the ability to control others. Firmness as well as mildness have characterized the spirit of the parental training. With such early influences, what but the well-poised governing power could be the out-come, a peculiar gift for the true teacher. Abundance of good sense and good nature is possessed by the Bicknells. Wise fools we have not in our households. God gave to every child of our race, five talents more or less, and his practical judgment, tact and skill have enabled him to make a gain on his capital in trade. Always hopeful, he has been the inspirer of hope and courage to others. Besides, the good teacher must possess his soul with *patience*, and did the wives or husbands of a Bicknell ever see one of the family *out of patience*. If so, I hope the case will be reported at our next re-union. These, and other qualities I have not time to mention, contribute a well balanced teaching character, and the men and women of our name who have taught at the home circle, and in the school-room in the days since Zachary, are many and distinguished.

Among those who have come under my own special notice, are, the many talented Quincy, our historian, of Hingham; the veteran William, of Buckfield, Maine; Simeon, the noted principal of a Vermont Academy, of an earlier day; Mrs. Ames, our accomplished poet of the day, now in Pennsylvania; Joshua Bicknell Chapin, of Rhode Island, teacher, physician, and lately State School Commissioner for several years; and if I may be allowed to refer to my own teaching life, I may say that I have taught in all grades of schools from primary to the college, have superintended the State schools of Rhode Island for nearly six years, and have published teachers' journals and magazines for nearly twenty years. It is a noted fact also, that *eight* of the ten children of one of our families have taught more or less successfully. These are but fractional parts of the great whole which includes some of the most talented, earnest and self-denying of our name. May our future record be more brilliant with the histories of those who at home or at school shall be the constant teachers of the true, the beautiful, and the good.

OUR ARTISTS.

The speaking canvas is eloquent; its language, universal, its immortality, sure. So may it prove with the distinguished art-masters and patrons of our name and descent.

RESPONSE BY MR. A. H. BICKNELL, OF MALDEN, MASS.

When Ball Hughes, the sculptor, came to this country, Andrew Jackson told him that he came fifty years too soon. To-day it is fifty years too soon to call for a response from "our artists." In art our family have "great expectations,"— we look to the future rather than to the dead past for great achievements. Buckle tells us that "As long as any man is engaged in collecting materials necessary for his own subsistence, there will be neither leisure nor taste for higher pursuits." With nations, great achievements in art never appear during the formative period — æsthetic development comes later. As with nations, so with the Bicknells!

That the true art instinct with the Bicknells is inherent, I cannot doubt. An accomplished artist informs me that many years ago while sketching in Switzerland, he made the acquaintance of a lady who painted in water-colors so much better than he that he was ashamed to show his own works in her presence. This lady was a daughter of the late Elhanan Bicknell, of London.

My lamented friend, William M. Hunt, declared that an art critic never was known to discover an original artist before he was forty; however that may be, a Bicknell discovered Turner, became his friend and patron thirty years before the peerless John Ruskin uttered a word in that renowned painter's praise. We have no great art achievements to record and dwell upon to-day, but later let the roll be called, the record be read and "honor to whom honor is due," let us then,

> "Bring Art to tremble nearer, touch enough
> The verge of vastness to inform our soul."

After the reading of several letters, the president called attention to the family coat of arms which had been painted in water colors by Harry Bicknell, and then introduced Mr. David Bicknell of New Jersey, of the London branch of the Bicknell family, who gave a short but interesting account of his family, and exhibited three portraits, of his grandfather William, his father William J., and his uncle Elhanan, the latter a gentleman of great wealth and a distinguished art-patron of London.

After a vote of thanks to the Committee of Arrangements and the appointment of a Publication Committee, consisting of

QUINCY BICKNELL,	MRS. CLARA B. WALKER,
THOMAS W. BICKNELL,	MRS. T. W. BICKNELL,
GEORGE A. BICKNELL,	MRS. E. B. CRANE,
ELLERY B. CRANE,	MRS. A. M. HOLLAND,
ROBERT T. BICKNELL.	MRS. GEO. W. BICKNELL,

the company joined in the singing of the following hymn composed by Mr. Alfred Bicknell.

CLOSING HYMN.

Tune — OLD HUNDRED.

I.

God of our fathers, 'twas Thy hand,
That o'er the seas to this broad land
Thy children led. — who reared the dome
Of this, our first New England home.

II.

Thy hand was o'er them, when Thy foes
Around their early altars rose :
Faith in Thy goodness and Thy power
Kept their hearts strong each trying hour.

III.

Unchanged, Thy hand is still our guide,
As we on Life's mysterious tide
Approach that bound in mercy given—
The eve of Life, the morn of Heaven.

IV.

To Thee, O God, our praise we give ;
In Thee, and only Thee, we live,
Past, present, future, still the same,
While worlds unnumbered bless Thy name.

V.

On us may grace and peace descend,
Faith never fail, love never end !
And take us, when this life is o'er,
Father, to Thee, for evermore.

At the close of these exercises. the family proceeded on foot and in carriages to view the site of the homestead of *our first parents*, Zachary and Agnes. Those possessed of vivid imaginations undoubtedly saw. or thought they saw. the old roof-tree. under which they lived. wrought and died. and the following lines written by another Bicknell bard testified to the devotion which the spot holds in his affections.

ZACHARY BICKNELL'S HOMESTEAD.

In sixteen hundred thirty-five or that time near,
Our Grandfather's Grandfather settled here.
We know not for certain, but believe 'tis the spot,
Where our Grandfather's Grandfather built him his cot.

And we his descendants have met here to day,
To bow at the shrine, where he used to pray;
And drop a loving tear on this dear old spot
Where our Grandfather's Grandfather built him his cot.

We have come, dear friends, from far, far away,
To spend in communion, this one short day;
And we trust the occasion will ne'er be forgot
That we spent where our Grandfather built him his cot.

And oh! may we carry away from here,
A loving regard for our Grandfather dear;
And may we be found to stand in our lot
As did our Grandfather, who died on this spot.

And now, dear friends, before we part,
Let each of us pledge, from our own true heart,
To keep in remembrance this day and this spot,
Where our Grandfather's Grandfather dwelt in his cot.

We are passing away, passing away,
Some of our friends going most every day;
Who of us may be called on the morrow
To leave fond, fond hearts, breaking with sorrow?

Let us be looking to mansions above
Where the just ever dwell in the presence of Love;
Where our Grandfather's Grandfather lives evermore,
Who went from this cot to the evergreen shore.

JOSEPH G. BICKNELL.

CAMBRIDGEPORT, Sept. 22, 1880.

From thence the party proceeded to King Oak Hill, a commanding eminence, near the fine residence of W. E. Bicknell. Here
the magnificent landscape and waterscape, with the long coast
line of Massachusetts Bay, from Nantasket Beach to Cape Ann,
were admired by all lovers of grandly picturesque scenery, while the
beauties were more carefully explored by the fine telescope of
Alfred Bicknell, and the points of historic interest were pointed
out and explained by Rev. Mr. Titus of the Weymouth Historical
Society. One of the attractions at King Oak Hill was W. E.
Bicknell's grapery, which offered a free lunch to all lovers of nice
fruits. After an hour spent in surveying the natural scenery of
Weymouth, Hingham, Abington, Braintree, Quincy, Dorchester,
Boston, the Blue Hills, the Atlantic, with its bays and harbors,
and all near and adjacent parts, the company proceeded to the Old
North Church, founded by the emigrants under Rev. Joseph Hull,
and thence to the cemetery, where " the forefathers of the village
sleep." Here among the old graves, were found slate-stone slabs,
to the memory of John Bicknell[3], Joseph[4] and Mary[5], with other
mounds, marked only by the autumn golden rod, and the evergreen junipers. Our thoughts were only filled with gratitude to
God that He gave to us so goodly an ancestry, while from the
heavens, may be, looked down and hovered near, the spirits of
those who were rejoicing in a posterity, not wholly unmindful of
the rich blessings flowing from such a heritage. One thought
lingered with us as we separated with hearty hand-shakings and
warm fraternal feelings from this first family re-union, that perhaps
on the two hundred and fiftieth anniversary of the year of our
American life as Bicknells, a thousand of our name and descent
might gather on that consecrated spot to erect a substantial monument in memory of

ZACHARY AND AGNES BICKNELL,

1635.

THE BICKNELLS.

The following list of names includes all those which have come to the knowledge of the officers of the Bicknell Family Association, and which have been enrolled as members. All persons who examine this list are urged to send to the Secretary, Mr. R. T. Bicknell, 200 Devonshire street, Boston, such other names as may be known to them. In this way the Association may be able to enter on its rolls, the names of all the living descendants of Zachary and Agnes Bicknell. Errors as well as omissions should be reported to the Secretary.

In the following list, the Christian names, only, are given.

BICKNELL.

A.

Angeline C.,	E. Dedham, Mass.
Abel,	Norwich, Vt.
Albion H.,	Malden, Mass.
Alden,	Foxboro, "
Alfred, 33 Milk St., Boston, and Melrose, Mass.	
A. B.,	26 Norton St., Albany, N. Y.
Allen D. B.,	New York City.
Alfred,	31 Mason St., Worcester, Mass.
Alfred,	Burlington, Vt.
Allen,	Underhill Centre, Vt.
Almond B.,	Gaylord, Smith Co., Kan.
Amos J.,	194 Broadway, N. Y. City.
Anson D.,	Humboldt, Iowa.
Allen,	Jericho, Vt.
Axel H.,	Minneapolis, Minn.

Albert P.,	Melrose, Mass.
Augustus M.,	No. Weymouth, Mass.
Ai,	Westford, Mass.
Alanson,	South Kingston, R. I.
Amos,	Westford, Mass.
Anson L.,	Weymouth, Mass.
Asa,	Lowell, Mass.

B.

Bennett,	Stanwix, N. Y.
Brownell M.,	
Benjamin,	Lamoille, Ill.
Byron,	Jericho, Vt.
Byron H.,	Kearney, Neb.
Byron J., 2 Howards Row, Memphis, Tenn.	
Betsy,	Genesee, N. Y.
Benjamin,	South Kingston, R. I.
Benjamin R.,	Bangor, Me.

C.

Chas. E., Rockland, Me.
Chas. C., McGregor, Iowa.
Chas. P., 3254 Chestnut St., Philadelphia, Pa.
Chas. H., Dr., Beloit, Wis.
Chas. F., Carson City, Nev.
Chas. H., Westford, Mass.
Chas. T., Massillon. Stark Co., Ohio
Chester C., Cedar Springs, Mich.
Caroline N., Boston Highlands.
Carlos B., Parishville, St. Lawrence Co., N. Y.
Chandler C., West Chesterfield, Mass.
Charles, North Weymouth, Mass.
Charles L., Weymouth, Mass.

D.

Dennis H., Rev., Underhill, Vt.
Daniel, Mrs., Hockingsport, Ohio.
Daniel, Mrs., Babylon, Suffolk Co., N. Y.
David, Brick Church, E. Orange, N. J.
Dana, Jericho, Vt.
Deborah, E. Dedham, Mass.
Dustin, Jericho, Vt.

E.

Edward, 43 Somerset St., Boston.
Edward, Lawrence, Mass.
Emery O., 5 Court Sq., Boston.
Emma R., 1 Oak St., Charlestown.
Edward, 397 Broadway, Albany, N. Y.
Ella, Waterford, N. Y.
Edward J., Box 227, Providence, R. I.
Elizabeth W., E. Dedham, Mass.
Elias P., 66 Front St., Worcester, Mass.
Elra, North Tunbridge, Vt.
Edna, Chelsea, Vt.
Ephraim, Windsor, Mass.
Ezra, Hingham, "
Ezra L., " "
Edward, 307 Hudson Ave., Albany, N. Y.
Emma E., Council Bluffs, Iowa.
Ella A., Springfield, Mass.
Edward, Providence, R. I.
Edwin, No. Weymouth, Mass.
Edward Q., New York City.

F.

Francis A., No. Weymouth, Mass.
Frank S., 55 High St., Worcester, Mass.
Franklin W., 63 No. Desplaines St., Chicago, Ill.
Frank J., 21 Carpenter St., Providence, R. I.

Frank A., Brockton, Mass.
Fred. A., Springfield, Mass.
Frank M., 34 Canal St., Boston.
Fred N., E. Weymouth, Mass.
Freeborn A., New York City.
Frank E., Canton, Me.
Frank H., Tunbridge, Vt.
Fred. J., Rev., Bangor, Me.

G.

Geo W., Rev., Lowell, Mass.
Geo. F., Attleboro, "
Geo. H., 57 Warren St., Boston Highlands.
Geo. J., 4 Summit St., Boston Highlands.
Geo. A., Box 3521, New York City.
Geo. A., New Albany, Ind.
Geo. E., No. Attleboro, Mass.
Geo. R., St. Louis Union Depot, St. Louis, Mo.
Geo., Underhill, Vt.
Geo. C., Jericho, Vt.
Geo. F., Wollaston, Mass.
Geo. H., Council Bluffs, Iowa.
Geo. H., Weymouth, Mass.
Geo E., 146 No. Colony St., Meriden, Conn.
Geo., 107 East 86th St., New York.
George S., Parishville, St. Lawrence Co., N. Y.

H.

Harriet, Canton, Me.
Henry S., Brockton, Mass.
Henry G., 127 Van Buren St., Chicago, Ill.
Henry F., E. Weymouth, Mass.
Harrison, No. " "
Henry A., Big Oak Flat, Cal.
Henry A., Buckfield, Me.
Henry C., " "
Homer, Dalton, Mass.
Henry T., No. Weymouth, Mass.
H. O., 63 No. Desplaines St., Chicago, Ill.
Hosea, Potsdam, N. Y.
Henry, Barrington, R. I.
Harrison C., Madison, N. Y.
Henry A., West Chesterfield, Mass.
Henry J., Newport, Me.
Hurlbert F., Lower California.

I.

Ira L., Jericho, Vt.
Ira, Westford, Mass.
I. J., Rev., Munroe, Adams Co., Ind.
Ida V., Mrs., Hingham, Mass.

J.

Joseph I., and his children, Henry P.,
  Pierrepont C., Joseph I., Eugene P.,
  Wm. A. P., Riverdale, New York
  City.
Japheth,   Smithfield, R. I.
James,   Providence, R. I.
James W.,   Canton, Me.
Joseph L.,   34 Green St., Boston, Mass.
James, Rev.,   Stanwix, N. Y.
John V., Buffalo Gen'l Hospital, Buffalo,
  N. Y.
James A.,   Brockton, Mass
J. Edward,   "   "
James F., 1186 Harrison Ave., Boston
  Highlands.
John Vinton,   Bristol, Vt.
James W.,   78 H St., So. Boston.
Jacob N. L.,   E. Weymouth, Mass
J. R., Rev.,   Muncie, Ind.
J. Bennett, 655 Case Ave., Cleveland, Ohio.
John,   West Paris, Me.
J. Otis,   Brockton, Mass.
James,   Lawrence, Mass.
John F.,   Worcester, Mass
John Stark,   Johnson, Vt.
Joseph G.,   Cambridgeport, Mass.
John H.,   West Chesterfield "
Jas. L.,   167 Broadway, N. Y
John,   26 Norton St., Albany, N. Y.
Jesse B.,   Providence, R. I.
Jesse,   24 Jenkins St.,   "   "
James,   East Providence, R. I.
James L.,   150 Beacon St., Prov., R. I.
Joseph P.,   Barrington, R. I.
Joshua,   Providence, R. I.
John Q.,   E. Weymouth, Mass.
John W.,   East Greenwich, R. I.
Joseph Hawley, 3254 Chestnut St., Phila-
  delphia, Pa.
Joseph,   375 Broadway, So. Boston.
James,   Cedar Springs, Mich.
James S.,   Newport, Me.
John H. Jr.,   West Chesterfield, Mass.
John James,   Patterson, Iowa.
John S.,   Lowell, Mass.
Joseph A.,   Maine.
Josiah,
Julius,   Lovington, Ill.

L.

Lucius,   Stanwix, N. Y.
Luke H.,   Gallatin, Tenn.
Luke Emerson, West Cummington, Mass.
Loammi,   Westford, Mass.
Lot W.,   No. Weymouth, Mass.
Lincoln B.,   Hingham, Mass.

M.

Moses,   Stanwix, N. Y.
Moses W.,   "   "
Mattie B.,   Auburn, Me.
Mary E., 307 Hudson Ave., Albany, N. Y.
Micajah,   Bicknell, Ind.
M. W., Rev.,   Bangor, Me.
Maude M.,   Melrose, Mass.
Martha A.,   Athens, Me.
Merrill L.,   Windsor, Mass.
Milo C.,   Patterson, Iowa.

N.

Nathaniel,   Canton, Me.
Nehemiah,   E. Greenwich, R. I.

O.

Otis P.,   Brookville, Kan.
Oscar,   Windsor, Mass.
Otis P.,   Beloit, Wis.
Orlando L., 63 No. Desplaines St., Chicago,
  Ill.
Oscar A.,   Bristol, Vt.
Otis C.,   Patterson, Iowa.
Otis C.,   Madison, N. Y.

P.

Preston F.,   Underhill, Vt.
Peter,   New Orleans, La.
Percy,   775 Tremont St., Boston.
Philip B.,   Lincoln, Eng.

Q.

Quincy,   Hingham, Mass.
Quincy L.,   E. Weymouth, Mass.
Quincy, jr.,   Lexington, Mass.

R.

Robert T., 200 Devonshire St., Boston, and
  E. Weymouth.
Robert T., 3254 Chestnut St., Philadelphia,
  Pa.
Raymond D.,   New York City.
Ralph A., Parishville, St. Lawrence Co.,
  N. Y.

S.

Stephen 2d,   No. Weymouth, Mass.
Samuel, Rev.,   Bedford, Ind.
Sarah F., Mrs., 46 So. Russell St., Boston,
  Mass.
Sumner H.,   Windsor, Mass.
Simeon,   Hebron, Me.
Simeon, Rev.,   —— Wisconsin.
Susan S., 97 Ebury St. Pimlico, London,
  England.

Sara,   Hallowell, Me.
Sanford,   Wisconsin.
Stephen,   North Weymouth, Mass.
Stephen A.,   "   "
Stephen K.,   Newport, Me.

T.

Thos. W , 16 Hawley St., Boston, and Dorchester, Mass.
Thos. W.,   East Greenwich, R. I.
Thos.,   No. Weymouth, Mass.
Thos. B., jr., 142 Broadway, N. Y.
Thos. B.,   Elizabeth, N. J.
Thaolin,   Sandwich, Mass.
Thomas M., Hannawa Falls, St. Lawrence
    Co., N. Y.
Tristam,   Buckfield, Me.

V.

Vesta, Mrs.,   Medina, Ohio.

W.

Walter F.,   117 Water St., Boston.

Wm.,   367 Dorchester St., South Boston.
Wm.,   Buckfield, Me.
Wm. E.,   43 Somerset St., Boston.
W. H. W.,   "   "   "
W. Wallace,   E. Dedham, Mass.
Wm. J., 4 Summit St., Boston Highlands.
Wm. C.,   Norwood, St. Law. Co., N. Y.
Wm.,   Norwich, Vt.
Wm. M., Rev.,   Rowe, Mass.
Wm. H.,   Providence, R. I.
Wm. E.,   Bristol, Vt.
William, 198 Raymond St., Brooklyn, N. Y.
Wesley, Mrs.,   Genesee, N. Y.
Wm. S.,   Bicknell, Ind.
Walter J.,   Providence, R. I.
William A.,   Smithfield, R. I.
William C., Louisville, St. Lawrence Co.
    N. Y.
William F.,   Newport, Me.

Z.

Zachariah L.,   E. Weymouth, Mass.

BICKNELL DESCENT.

A.

Adams, Rev. W. W., D. D., Fall River, Mass.
Ager, George B.,   City Hall, Boston.
Allen, Mrs. Lucius,   Canton, Me.
    " Daniel B.,   New York City.
Ames, Mrs. A. H.,   Columbia, Pa.
Atterbury, Frank,   New York.
    " Frederick,   "   "
Atwood, William O.,   Newton, Mass.
Austin, Samuel,   Vassalboro', Me.
    " William,   "   "

B.

Bennett, Jane B., 764 River St. Troy, N. Y.
Bowles, Mrs. Roxanna, So. Weymouth, Mass.
Bennet, S. W.,   Abington, Mass.
Bates, Eliel,   So. Hingham, Mass.
Becker, Mrs. C. B., Middleburgh, N. Y.
Babcock, Mrs. Augusta, West Derby, Liverpool, Eng.

Burnett, Merriel L., Savoy Centre, Mass.
Bowman, Mrs. J. A., Berwick Park Bost'n
Brown, Emily, 97 Ebury St. Pimlico, London, England.
Bates, Lovell B.,   E. Weymouth, Mass.
    " Mrs. Edmund G.,   "   "
    " Mrs. Leavitt,   "   "
    " Amos,   "   "
    " Francis B.,   "   "
    " Alpheus,   "   "
Blanchard, Theodore, No. Weymouth, Mass.
Blanchard, Cornelius F., No. Weymouth, Mass.
Blanchard, Fletcher G., No. Weymouth, Mass.
Blanchard, Edward R., No. Weymouth, Mass.
Burrell, Mrs. Quincy, No. Weymouth, Mass
Burrell, Mrs. Anna, East Weymouth, Mass.

Benham, Mrs. James D., South Colton, St. Lawrence Co., N. Y.
Bryant, Mrs. Deborah, Ohio.
Beal, Mrs. Emily F., No. Weymouth, Mass.
Burr, Mrs. Caroline, Attleborough, Mass.
Bates, Alfred L., Hingham, Mass.
" John W., East Weymouth, Mass.
" Mrs. Anna, " " "
" Amos B., Hingham, Mass.
" Urban S., " "
Blossom, Mrs. Caroline L., Roxbury, Mass.
Buck, Mrs. Emeline, Providence, R. I.
Bracket, Mrs. Frank, Bloomfield, Me.
" Charles, " "

C.

Chamberlain, Mrs. M. A., 20 St. James St., Boston Highlands.
Culbertson, Mrs. John C. New Albany, Ind.
Culbertson, Emma V. P. B., 3613 Locust St. Philadelphia, Pa.
Cushman, Wm., Buckfield, Me.
Cowan, Mrs. C. H., Fremont, Neb.
Crane, Ellery B., Worcester, Mass.
Cooper, Mrs. Olive, Belfast, Me.
Chapin, Joshua B., Providence, R. I.
Chapman, Mrs. Eliza L., " "
" Mrs. Mary Fitch, Westerly, R. I.
Cowing, Mrs. F. H., E. Weymouth, Mass.
Cain, Mrs. Elizabeth P., E. Weymouth, Mass.
Clapp, Mrs. Harriet, Weymouth, Mass.
" Henry, " "
" Horace, " "
Clive, Sophronia A., Poughkeepsie, N. Y.
Campbell, Mrs. Lilleyons, Hingham, Mass.
Crandall, Mrs. George, Pierpont, N. Y.
Cowing, Frank, East Weymouth, Mass.
" Mrs. Ella, " "
Cushing, Mrs. Henry, No. Weymouth, Mass.
Cassler, Mrs. Kate C., Fonda, N. Y.
Conant, Mrs. Dela W. Willimantic, Conn.
Chapin, Mrs Eliza, Taunton, Mass.
Chesborough, Mrs. Sarah, Wrentham, Mass.
Cheever, Mrs. Maria, New York.
Crocket, Mrs. Chas. H., Stetson, Me.
Crawford, Mrs. Lucy Ella, Oakland, Cal.

D.

Dickinson, Mrs. Nancy, Westerly, R. I.
De Coster Mrs. Isabelle, Holbrook. Mass.
Davy, Mrs. Geo., Hebron, Me.
DeCoster, W. K., Canton, Me.
Dixon, Mrs. Rev. Hiram, Ripon, Wis.

Dickinson, Rufus W., Providence, R. I.
" Wm. G., New Haven, Conn.
Denton, Mrs. Marinda D., E. Weymouth, Mass.
Davis, Mrs. Anna T., Roxbury, Mass.
" William A., Hartford, Me.
Draper, Mrs. Anna, Attleborough, Mass.
Dawes, Mrs. Eliza, Providence, R. I.
Dodge, Henry B., Newport, Me.

E.

Evans, Mrs. T. J., E. Weymouth, Mass.

F.

Franklin, Benj., Rev., Shrewsbury, N. J.
Foster, Isa B., Bates College, Lewiston, Me.
Forbes, Mrs. Julia C., Buckfield, Me.
Foot, Mrs. E. B., Medina, Ohio.
Forbes, Mrs Almira, Neponset, Mass.
Fardy, Mrs. James M., Auburn, Me.
Fuller, Mrs. L. A., Jericho, Vt.
Foote, Nancy E., Cleveland, Ohio.
Folsom, Esther O., Tunbridge, Vt.
Fisk, Mrs. Rufus H., West Chesterfield, Mass.
Forbes, John H., Neponset, Mass.
" Willard, " "
" Howard, " "
Fletcher, Mrs. H. Q., Hingham, Mass.
French, Frank W., East Weymouth, Mass.
" Stephen, " " "
" William T., " " "
Fowle, Mrs. Rebecca, Canton, Me.
Franklin, Edward, Providence, R. I.
Fisher, Mrs. Frances A., Newport, Me.
Fuller, Mrs. Wm. G., Newport, Me.
" Mrs. Edna, Underhill, Vt.
Freeman George, Lisle, N. Y.
" Edwin, " "
" Albert D., " "
" Charles, " "
" Elijah, New York.
" Lewis, " "
" Norman A., Mansfield, Conn.
French, Mrs. Peter W., E. Weymouth, Mass.
French, Mrs. Waldo C., E. Weymouth, Mass.
French, Mrs. Jacob, E. Weymouth, Mass.
" Mrs. Lucinda B., E. Weymouth, Mass.

G.

Gage, Sarah B., 307 Hudson Ave., Albany, N. Y.
Gorgas, Mrs. Dr. A. C., care C. P. Bicknell, 3254 Chestnut St., Phila., Pa.

Viall, Amy B., East Providence, R. I.
" Elizabeth B., " " "
" Mrs. Elizabeth, " " "

W.

Walker, Mrs. Clara B., 9 Chestnut St., Lynn, Mass.
Watson, Matthew, Welcome, P. O., St. James Parish, La.
Watson, Samuel, Nashville, Tenn.
Watson, Wm. P., 1337 Corcoran St., Washington, D. C.
Wade, Frank L., Athens, Me.
Whitthorne, Mrs. R., 1337 Corcoran St. Washington, D. C.
Wheeler, Samuel G., New York, N. Y.
Wyman, Rev. Edwin A., Leominster, Mass.
Wheeler, Mrs. Mary, Providence, R. I.
Weeks, Mrs. Nancy B., Paris, Oneida Co., N. Y.

Whitney, Edw. P., Westfield, N. Y.
Whittemore, Mrs. Margaret, Attleborough, Mass.
Wheeler, James M., Boston, Mass.
" Thomas M., " "
" Mrs. Mary, Canton, Me.
" Edward B., " "
" George M., Boston, Mass.
Wood, Mrs. Ancil, Newport, Me.
" " Isaac, Stetson, "
Wyman, Albert, Bloomfield, Me.
" Charles A., " "
White, Mrs. Palmer, Newport, Me.
" George E., " "
Welch, Mrs. Henry A., S. Colton, St. Law. Co., N. Y.
Wilder, Mrs. William C., Hingham, Mass.

Y.

Young, Dr. S. B., Salt Lake City, Utah.
Young, Mrs. Harriet K., Providence, R. I.
Young, Mrs. Joseph, Salt Lake City, Utah.

www.ingramcontent.com/pod-product-compliance
Lightning Source LLC
Chambersburg PA
CBHW032204010726
47493CB00008BA/2826